# THE VOYAGES OF
# DOCTOR
# DOLITTLE

# THE VOYAGES OF
# DOCTOR DOLITTLE

### TOLD AND ILLUSTRATED BY
## HUGH LOFTING
### ADAPTED FOR YOUNGER READERS
### BY N. H. KLEINBAUM

## A YEARLING BOOK

Published by
Bantam Doubleday Dell Books for Young Readers
a division of
Bantam Doubleday Dell Publishing Group, Inc.
1540 Broadway
New York, New York 10036

If you purchased this book without a cover you should be aware that
this book is stolen property. It was reported as "unsold and destroyed"
to the publisher and neither the author nor the publisher has received
any payment for this "stripped book."

Copyright, 1922, by Hugh Lofting
Copyright, 1950, by Josephine Lofting
Revised edition copyright © 1988 by Christopher Lofting
Adaptation edition copyright © 1997 by Bantam Doubleday Dell
Books for Young Readers

All rights reserved. No part of this book may be reproduced or transmit-
ted in any form or by any means, electronic or mechanical, including
photocopying, recording, or by any information storage and retrieval
system, without the written permission of the Publisher, except where
permitted by law.

The trademarks Yearling® and Dell® are registered in the U.S. Patent
and Trademark Office and in other countries.

ISBN: 0-440-41240-4
Printed in the United States of America
March 1997
CWO 10 9 8 7 6 5 4 3 2

# TO COLIN
# AND ELIZABETH

# CONTENTS

## PART V

## PART VI

# PROLOGUE

A great deal of what I have written so far about Doctor Dolittle took place before I was born. But I am now writing about that part of the great man's life that I myself saw and took part in.

Many years ago the Doctor gave me permission to do this. But we were both so busy then, having adventures and filling notebooks full of natural history, that I never seemed to have time to sit down and write of our doings.

Now, of course, I am quite an old man and my memory isn't so good anymore. But whenever I am in doubt, I always ask Polynesia, the parrot.

That wonderful bird (she is now nearly two hundred and fifty years old) sits on the top of my desk, usually humming sailor songs to herself, while I write this book. And as everyone who has ever met her knows, Polynesia's memory is the most marvelous memory in the world.

First of all, I must tell you something about myself and how I came to meet the Doctor.

# Part I

*I would sit on the river wall with my feet
dangling over the water.*

# THE COBBLER'S SON

My name is Tommy Stubbins. I am the son of Jacob, the cobbler of Puddleby-on-the-Marsh. When I was nine and a half years old, Puddleby was a small town with a river running through it. Over the river was an old stone bridge called Kingsbridge, which led from the marketplace to the churchyard on the other side.

Sailing ships came up the river and anchored near the bridge. I would sit on the river wall with my feet dangling over the water, watching the sailors as they worked and pretending I was a sailor too.

I longed to sail with the ships when they left Puddleby. I wanted to go out into the world to seek my fortune and see foreign lands.

I had three great friends in Puddleby. One was Joe, the mussel man, who lived in a tiny hut by the edge of the water under the bridge. He made wonderful things with his hands and mended my toy ships for me.

Sometimes Joe would take me out in his boat. We would paddle down the river as far as the edge of the sea to get mussels and lobsters to sell. Out there on the cold, lonely marshes we saw wild geese, curlews, redshanks and many other seabirds.

Another friend was Matthew Mugg, the cat's-meat man. He was a funny old person with a bad squint. He looked rather awful but was nice to talk to. He knew everybody in Puddleby. People paid him to give meat to their cats and dogs.

The cats and dogs ran to the garden gates whenever they heard Matthew calling. I would go with Matthew, and sometimes he let me give the meat to the animals. He knew a lot about dogs and would tell me the names of different kinds.

My third great friend was Luke the Hermit. But I will tell you more about him later on.

I did not go to school because my father was not rich enough to send me. But I loved animals. I spent my time collecting birds' eggs and butterflies, blackberries and mushrooms; fishing in the river; and helping the mussel man mend his nets.

It was a pleasant life, though of course I did not think so then. Like all boys, I wanted to grow up in a hurry. I did not know how lucky I was with nothing to worry me. I could not wait for the day when I could leave my father's house and sail down the river and out into the world to seek my fortune.

# I HEAR OF THE GREAT NATURALIST

One early morning in the springtime, I was wandering among the hills and came upon a hawk with a squirrel in his claws.

The squirrel fought very hard for his life. The hawk was so frightened when he saw me that he dropped the squirrel and flew away. I picked up the poor animal and found that two of his legs were badly hurt. I quickly carried him back to town.

I went straight to the mussel man's hut near the bridge. Joe put on his glasses and examined the animal carefully, shaking his head.

"Yon crittur's got a broken leg," he said. "And the other leg is badly cut. I can mend your boats, Tom, but I don't know how to fix a broken squirrel. This is a job

*I came upon a hawk with a squirrel in his claws.*

for a surgeon—and a right smart one too. There be only one man I know who could save yon crittur's life. And that's John Dolittle."

"Who is John Dolittle?" I asked. "Is he a vet?"

"No," said Joe. "He's no vet. Doctor Dolittle is a natcheralist! He knows all about animals and butterflies and plants and rocks. I'm surprised you never heard of him! He knows a whole lot about shellfish, too. He's a quiet man. But folks say he's the greatest natcheralist in the whole world."

"Where does he live?"

"Over on the Oxenthorpe Road, on the other side of town. Go see him. He's a great man."

"Thank you, Joe," I said, taking the poor squirrel in my arms and starting toward the Oxenthorpe Road.

"Meat! *M-E-A-T!*" I heard, as I came into the market-place.

"There's Matthew Mugg," I said to myself. "He'll know where this doctor lives. He knows everyone." I hurried across the marketplace and caught up with him.

"Matthew," I called. "Do you know Doctor Dolittle?"

"Do I know John Dolittle?" he said. "I should think I do! He's a very great man."

"Can you show me where he lives?" I asked.

"Certainly," he said with a smile. "I'm on my way to his house now.

"I've known John Dolittle for years," Matthew added as we left the marketplace. "But I'm pretty sure he ain't home now. He's away on a voyage. He'll be back any day. I'll show you his house and then you'll know where to find him."

All the way down the Oxenthorpe Road, Matthew hardly stopped talking about his great friend, Doctor John Dolittle.

"Where did the Doctor go on his voyage?" I asked.

"I couldn't tell you," Matthew said. "Nobody never knows where he goes, when he's going or when he's coming back. He lives all alone except for his pets. He's made great voyages and wonderful discoveries. As for animals, well, there ain't no one knows as much about 'em as he does."

"How did he get to know so much about animals?"

The cat's-meat man stopped and leaned down to whisper in my ear. *"He talks their language,"* he said in a hoarse, mysterious voice.

"The animals' language?" I cried.

"Why, certainly," said Matthew. "All animals have some kind of language. Some talk more than others; some speak only in sign language. But the Doctor understands them all—birds as well as animals. We keep it a secret, though, because folks only laugh when you speak of it. He can even *write* animal language! He's now busy learning the language of the shellfish. But he says it's hard work, and he's caught some bad colds, holding his head underwater so much."

"I do wish he were home so I could meet him," I said.

"Well, there's his house," said the cat's-meat man. "That little one at the bend of the road."

We were at the very edge of town. The house Matthew pointed to was a small one, standing by itself. There was a big garden around it. There were many fine fruit trees in the garden, but the wall was so high I couldn't see anything else.

When we reached the house, Matthew went up to the front gate, which was locked. A dog came running down from the house. The cat's-meat man pushed some meat and bags of corn and bran through the bars of the gate. The dog did not stop to eat the meat. Instead, he took all the things back into the house. He had a strange, shiny, wide collar around his neck. Matthew turned and went back down the steps. I followed him.

"The Doctor isn't back yet," he said, "or the gate wouldn't be locked."

"What were all those things in paper bags you gave the dog?"

"Oh, those were things for the animals to eat," Matthew explained. "The Doctor's house is full of pets. I give the things to the dog while the Doctor's away and he gives them to the other animals."

"And what was that strange collar he was wearing?"

"That's a solid gold dog collar," said Matthew. "It was given to him when he was with the Doctor on one of his voyages long ago. He saved a man's life."

"How long has the Doctor had him?"

"Oh, a long time. Jip's getting pretty old. That's why the Doctor doesn't take him on his voyages anymore. He leaves him behind to take care of the house. Jip never lets anyone come inside the garden while the

Doctor's away—not even me. You'll always be able to tell when the Doctor's back because if he is, the gate is always open."

I thanked Matthew and went home. I put my squirrel to bed in an old wooden box full of straw. I decided to take care of him myself until the Doctor returned.

Every day I went to the house with the big garden and tried the gate to see if it was locked. Sometimes the dog, Jip, would come down to see me. But although he always wagged his tail and seemed glad to see me, he never let me come inside the garden.

# THE DOCTOR'S HOME

One April afternoon, I thought I would see if the Doctor had come back yet. My squirrel wasn't getting any better, and I was worried about him.

I started toward the Doctor's house. On the way, it began to look as though it might rain.

I reached the gate. It was locked, and I felt very discouraged. I had come every day for a week. I was worried that my squirrel would die before the Doctor came back. I turned away and headed home.

Suddenly rain began to pour down. It got dark, almost like night. The wind blew. Thunder rolled. Lightning flashed. In a moment the gutters on the side of the road flowed like a river. There was no place to take shelter, so I started to run home.

I hadn't gone far when I bumped into something soft and fell. When I looked up, sitting on the wet pavement near me was a little round man with a kind face. He wore a shabby high hat and carried a small black bag.

"I'm very sorry," I apologized. "I had my head down and didn't see you coming."

Instead of getting angry, the little man began to laugh.

"It was just as much my fault as yours, you know," he said, smiling. "I had my head down too—but we mustn't sit talking like this. We're soaked. How far do you have to go?"

"To the other side of town," I said.

"Come to my house and get dried. A storm like this can't last."

We ran back down the road together. I wondered who this funny man could be and where he lived. I was a stranger to him and here he was taking me to his own home to get dried!

"Here we are," he said.

I looked up and found myself at the foot of the steps leading to the little house with the big garden. My friend was running up the steps to the gate with some keys.

*Surely,* I thought, *this cannot be the great Doctor Dolittle himself!*

I suppose after hearing so much about him, I had expected someone very tall and strong. It was hard to believe that Doctor Dolittle was this little man with the kind face. Yet here he was, opening the gate where I had waited for so many days.

The dog, Jip, came rushing out, barking with happiness.

"Are you Doctor Dolittle?" I shouted as we raced up the short garden path to the house.

"Yes," he said, opening the front door with the keys. "Now get in! Don't worry about wiping your feet. Never mind the mud."

I popped in, he and Jip followed and he slammed the door.

"My goodness! What a storm!"

The storm had made it dark outside, but inside, with the door closed, it was black as night. Suddenly I heard a strange noise, like all kinds of animals and birds squeaking and screeching at once. I heard things hurrying down stairs and along passageways. I felt birds' wings fluttering near my face. Things kept bumping into my legs. I was becoming a bit scared when I felt the Doctor take hold of my arm and shout into my ear.

"Don't be alarmed! These are just some of my pets. I've been away three months. They're glad to see me home again. Stand still while I strike a light."

I stood in the pitch black while all kinds of animals I couldn't see chattered around me. It seemed like a weird dream.

"My matches are all wet. Have you got any?" the Doctor called to me.

"No, I haven't," I called back.

"Never mind," he said. "Perhaps Dab-Dab can raise us a light somewhere."

The Doctor made some funny clicking noises with his tongue. I heard someone climb the stairs again and start moving about in the rooms above.

After a minute I saw the glimmerings of light on the landing above. The animals were silent.

"I thought you lived alone," I said to the Doctor.

"I do," he said. "It is Dab-Dab who is bringing the light."

I looked up the stairs. The strange-sounding footsteps grew louder, sounding like someone hopping from step to step on one leg.

"Ah—at last! Good old Dab-Dab!" cried the Doctor.

And then I thought I *really* must be dreaming. Craning her neck around the bend of the landing, hopping on one leg, came a spotless white duck. And in her right foot she carried a lighted candle!

*And in her right foot she carried a lighted candle!*

# THE WIFF-WAFF

The hall was full of animals. The Doctor took the candlestick from the duck and turned to me.

"You must get those wet clothes off. By the way, what is your name?"

"Tommy Stubbins," I said.

"The son of Jacob Stubbins, the shoemaker?"

"Yes," I said.

"Excellent bootmaker, your father," said the Doctor. "You see these?" He held up the boot on his enormous right foot. "Your father made these four years ago, and I've been wearing them ever since. Well now, Stubbins, you've got to change those wet things. You can wear an old suit of mine until yours dries by the fire."

More candles were lit around the house. We went upstairs into a bedroom. The Doctor opened a wardrobe and took out two suits of old clothes, and we put them on. We carried our wet clothes down to the kitchen and started a fire in the big chimney. The Doctor's coat was so big on me, I kept stepping on the coattails while helping to get wood from the cellar. Soon we had a huge fire burning.

"Now let's cook some supper," said the Doctor. "You'll stay and have supper, of course?"

I was beginning to be very fond of this funny little man who treated me like a grown-up friend. When he asked me to have supper with him, I felt terribly proud and happy. But I suddenly remembered that I had not told my mother I would be late.

"Thank you very much. I would like to stay, but I'm afraid my mother would worry if I don't get back."

"Oh, but my dear Stubbins," said the Doctor, "your clothes aren't dry yet. You'll have to wait for them. By the time they are ready, we'll have supper cooked and eaten."

The Doctor felt around inside his bag. First he pulled out a loaf of new bread. Then came a glass jar with a strange top to it. He held this up to the light very carefully before he set it on the table. I could see an odd little water creature swimming about inside. At last the Doctor brought out a pound of sausages.

"Now," he said, "all we want is a frying pan."

We went into the kitchen, where pots and pans hung from the wall. The Doctor reached for a frying pan.

While he cooked, I went to look at the creature swimming in the glass jar.

"What is this animal?" I asked.

"That's a wiff-waff," said the Doctor. "Its proper name is *Hippocampus pippitopitus*. But the natives just call it a wiff-waff, because of the way it waves its tail to swim, I imagine. That's why I went on this last voyage. I'm trying to learn the language of the shellfish."

"Why?" I asked.

"Some of the shellfish are the oldest animals in the world. If I could talk their language I could learn a whole lot about what the world was like ages ago."

We sat at the kitchen table to eat. It was a wonderful kitchen. It was very cozy, homelike and warm. The fireplace was like a room in itself. You could get right inside it, even when the logs were burning, and sit on the wide seats on either side and roast chestnuts, listen to the kettle singing, tell stories, or look at picture books by the light of the fire. It was just like the Doctor— comfortable, sensible, friendly and solid.

While we were gobbling away, the door opened. In marched the duck, Dab-Dab, and the dog, Jip, dragging sheets and pillowcases behind them over the clean tiled floor.

Seeing my look of surprise, the Doctor explained, "They're just going to air the bedding for me in front of the fire. Dab-Dab is a treasure of a housekeeper. She never forgets anything."

The Doctor said a few words to the dog and the duck in some strange talk and signs. They seemed to understand him perfectly.

"Can you talk in squirrel language?" I asked.

"Oh, yes, that's quite an easy language," said the Doctor. "You could learn that without a great deal of trouble. Why do you ask?"

I told the Doctor about the squirrel I had rescued from the hawk. "Could you look at him tomorrow?"

"Well, if his leg is badly broken I think I had better see him tonight. It may be too late to do much, but I'll come home with you and take a look at him."

We felt the clothes by the fire. Mine were dry, and I changed in the bedroom. When I came down, the Doctor was waiting for me with his little black bag full of medicines and bandages.

"Come along," he said. "The rain has stopped now."

Outside it had grown quite bright again. Thrushes were singing in the garden as we opened the gate to go down onto the road.

# POLYNESIA

"I think your house is the most interesting one I was ever in," I said as we walked. "May I come again tomorrow?"

"Certainly," said the Doctor. "Come any day you like. Tomorrow I'll show you the garden and my private zoo. The larger animals are in a zoo in the garden because they are too big for the house."

"It must be splendid to be able to talk all the languages of the different animals," I said. "Do you think I could ever learn to do it?"

"Oh, surely," said the Doctor, "with practice and patience. You really ought to have Polynesia teach you. She gave me my first lessons."

"Who is Polynesia?"

"She is a West African parrot. She isn't with me any-more now," the Doctor said sadly.

"Is she dead?"

"Oh, no," the Doctor said. "She is still living, I hope. But when we reached Africa she seemed so glad to be back in her own country. When I had to return I could not bear to take her away—although she did offer to come. I left her in Africa. I have missed her. She's one of the best friends I ever had. She gave me the idea of learning animal languages and becoming an animal doctor."

At that moment we heard the sound of someone running behind us. We turned and saw Jip, the dog. He started barking and whining to the Doctor in a peculiar way. Then the Doctor got excited and began talking and making signs to Jip.

"Polynesia has come back!" he said, turning to me, his face shining with happiness. "Imagine! Jip says she has just returned to the house. It's been five years since I've seen her. Excuse me a minute."

He turned toward home. But the parrot, Polynesia, was flying toward us. She headed straight to the Doctor's shoulder and immediately began talking a steady stream in a language I could not understand. Soon the Doctor forgot all about me, my squirrel, Jip and everything else.

"Oh, excuse me, Stubbins," said the Doctor. "We must get on and see your squirrel. Polynesia, this is Thomas Stubbins."

The parrot nodded gravely. To my great surprise, in perfect English she said, "How do you do? I remember the night you were born."

"Stubbins is anxious to learn animal language," the Doctor said. "I was just telling him about you and the lessons you gave me."

"Well," said the parrot, "I never could have done it if he hadn't first taught me what *I* was saying when I spoke English. Many parrots can talk like a person, but few understand what they're saying."

As we approached my house, Jip ran in front of us. Polynesia perched on the Doctor's shoulder. She chattered on in English about Africa.

"How is Prince Bumpo getting on?" the Doctor asked.

"I almost forgot to tell you!" Polynesia said. *"Bumpo is in England!"*

"What on earth is he doing here?" cried the Doctor.

"His father, the King, sent him here to a place called, er, Bullford, I think it was, to study lessons."

"Bullford?" muttered the Doctor. "I never heard of the place. . . . Oh, you mean Oxford!"

"Yes, that's the place—Oxford. I knew it had something to do with cattle."

"Well, well," murmured the Doctor. "Fancy Bumpo studying at Oxford."

"There were great doings in Jolliginki when he left," Polynesia said. "He was scared to death to come. But his father said all the African kings were sending their sons abroad to study and he must go."

"And how is Chee-Chee?"

The Doctor explained to me that Chee-Chee was his pet monkey, who had also stayed behind in Africa.

"Well," said Polynesia, "Chee-Chee is not happy. He was homesick for you and the house and the garden. I was the same way myself. I couldn't settle down, even though I was glad to be in Africa. One night I made up my mind that I'd come back here and find you. I hunted up old Chee-Chee and told him. He said he didn't blame me. Africa was so very quiet after the life we led here with you. He missed your stories and our chats around the fire at night.

"When I left, Chee-Chee broke down and cried. He said it wasn't fair that he didn't have wings. But I'll bet he finds some way back. He's a smart lad."

We reached my home. My father's shop was closed and the shutters were up, but my mother was standing at the door looking up and down the street.

"Good evening, Mrs. Stubbins," the Doctor said. "I'm sorry your son is so late. We ran into one another in the storm. I made him stay to supper while his clothes dried."

"I was beginning to worry about him," my mother said. "Thank you, sir, for looking after him and bringing him home. And who might it be that I have the honor of addressing?" she asked, looking at Polynesia on the Doctor's shoulder.

"Oh, I'm John Dolittle. I imagine your husband will remember me. He made me some excellent boots about four years ago," the Doctor said.

"The Doctor has come to cure my squirrel, Mother," I said. "He knows all about animals."

"Oh, no, not all about them, Stubbins, by any means," the Doctor said, smiling shyly.

"It is kind of you to come so far to look after his pet," my mother said. "Tom is always bringing home strange creatures from the woods and fields."

"Is he?" said the Doctor. "Perhaps he will grow up to be a naturalist someday!"

"Won't you come in?" asked my mother.

"Thank you," said the Doctor. "What a charming home you have!"

And after wiping his huge boots carefully on the mat, the great man went into my house.

# THE WOUNDED SQUIRREL

Inside, my father was practicing the flute. The Doctor immediately started talking about flutes and other musical instruments he played.

"Won't you play us a tune?" my father asked.

"Well," said the Doctor, "it's been a long time, but I'd like to try. May I?"

The Doctor put the flute to his lips. He was wonderful! My mother and father and even I sat still, as though we were in church.

"That was lovely," my mother sighed as he finished.

"You are a great musician, sir," my father said.

The Doctor smiled. "I've nearly forgotten about the squirrel, and it is getting late," he said.

"I'll show him to you." I led the Doctor up the stairs to my room.

When the Doctor came in, the animal sat up at once and started to chatter.

Doctor Dolittle answered, and the squirrel seemed happy, rather than scared, as the Doctor examined him. I held a candle as the Doctor tied the leg in splints made of matchsticks.

"I think you will find that his leg will get better in a very short time," the Doctor said. "Don't let him run about for at least two weeks. Keep him in the open air and cover him with dry leaves if the nights are cool. He misses his wife and family. I will have a squirrel from my garden bring him news of them. He will be all right."

We went back to the parlor, where the Doctor played the flute for my mother and father late into the night.

# SHELLFISH TALK

The next morning I was up early even though I had gone to bed so late. I jumped out of bed into my clothes. I could hardly wait to go see the Doctor and his private zoo. I crept on tiptoe down the stairs and raced into the empty, silent street.

When I got to the Doctor's gate, I suddenly thought I might be too early. I peeked into the garden. No one was about. I quietly opened the gate and went inside.

I turned to go down a path between some hedges. "Good morning. How early you are!" I heard a voice quite close to me call. I turned and saw Polynesia sitting on top of a hedge.

"Good morning. I hope I'm not too early. Is the Doctor still in bed?"

Polynesia laughed. "He's been up for hours. The front door is open. He's probably making breakfast or in his study. I'm waiting to see the sun rise," the parrot said. "But this awful climate! In Africa the world would be blazing with sunlight! Here the mist is rolling over the cabbages. I don't know why anything but frogs ever stays in England."

I opened the front door and went into the kitchen, where a large kettle boiled on the fire. Bacon and eggs sat on a dish on the hearth.

I found the Doctor in the study surrounded by telescopes, microscopes and all sorts of things I did not understand but wished I did. Hanging on the walls were pictures of animals, fish and strange plants, and there were birds' eggs and seashells in glass cases.

The Doctor was standing at the main table in his dressing gown. At first I thought he was washing his face. He had a square glass box before him full of water, and he was holding one ear under the water while he covered the other with his hand.

"Good morning, Stubbins. Nice day, don't you think?" said the Doctor. "I've just been listening to the wiff-waff. Very disappointing."

"Didn't you find that he has any language at all?" I asked.

"Oh, he has a language. But such a poor language—only a few words, like *yes* and *no, hot* and *cold.*"

"I suppose that means he hasn't very much sense, if he only knows a few words," I said.

"Possibly it's the kind of life he leads," the Doctor said. "Wiff-waffs are very rare and solitary. They swim alone in the deepest parts of the ocean, so they don't really need to talk much."

"Perhaps some kind of a bigger shellfish would talk more," I suggested.

"Yes," said the Doctor. "I'm sure there are shellfish who are good talkers. But the biggest of them are so hard to catch. They're found in the deep parts of the sea, and they don't swim much. I do wish I could find some way to go to the bottom of the sea. I could learn a lot. But I shall manage it someday. Have you had breakfast yet, Stubbins?"

# "ARE YOU A GOOD NOTICER?"

olynesia came into the room while we were having breakfast and said something to the Doctor in bird language. At once he put down his knife and fork and left the room.

"You know, it's an awful shame," said the parrot when the Doctor closed the door. "As soon as he comes home, animals all over the countryside hear of it, and every sick cat and mangy rabbit comes to see him for his advice. Now there's a big fat hare outside at the back door with a squawking baby. Can she see the Doctor, please! The animals are *so* inconsiderate. The poor man never gets any peace!"

"Why don't the animals see other doctors?" I asked.

"Oh, good gracious," cried the parrot scornfully. "There aren't any other animal doctors—not real doctors. Oh, of course there *are* those vet persons. But they're no good. They can't understand animal language. Imagine if you went to a doctor who couldn't understand a word you said. How could he tell you to get well?"

"Do you think I could ever learn the languages of the animals?" I asked.

"Well, it depends," Polynesia said. "Are you clever at lessons?"

"I don't know," I admitted, feeling ashamed. "I've never been to school. My father is too poor."

"Well," said the parrot, "from what I have seen of schoolboys, I don't think you've missed much! But are you a good noticer? Being a good noticer is terribly important. For instance, if you saw two cock starlings on an apple tree, and took only one good look at them, would you be able to tell one from the other if you saw them the next day?"

"I don't know," I said. "I've never tried."

"Well, that," said the parrot, "is what you call powers of observation—noticing the small things about birds and animals: the way they walk, move their heads, flip their wings. Or the way they sniff the air, twitch their whiskers and wiggle their tails.

"You'll have to be patient," she continued. "It takes a long time to say even a few words right. But if you come

*Being a good noticer is terribly important.*

here often, I'll give you lessons myself. It would be good if you could learn because then you could help the Doctor. That is, if you are really interested in animals."

"Oh, I'd love that!" I cried. "Do you think the Doctor would let me?"

"Certainly, as soon as you have learned something of doctoring. I'll speak to him myself. Shhh! Here he comes. Bring back his plate from the hearth!"

# THE GARDEN OF DREAMS

**A**fter breakfast the Doctor showed me the garden. It was hard to see how big it really was. Just when you thought you'd seen it all, you would turn a corner and there was a whole new part.

It had everything. There were wide lawns with carved stone seats and old flagged paths with high yew hedges that looked like narrow streets. Doorways had been made through the hedges and were shaped like vases, peacocks and half-moons. A marble fishpond glistened with carp, water lilies and big frogs.

There were also summerhouses, one filled with books. There was an outdoor fireplace, where the Doctor liked to fry liver and bacon and eat in the open air. A couch on wheels allowed him to sleep under any tree and listen to nightingales singing. But best of all was a tiny tree house high in the branches of a great elm with a long rope ladder, where the Doctor went to look at the moon and stars through a telescope. It was a garden you could explore endlessly.

There were a lot of birds in the garden. Every tree had nests. Green lizards and snakes also wiggled around the garden.

"Why do all these different animals come and live here?" I asked.

"Well, I guess it's because they get the food they like and nobody worries or hurts them. And, of course, they know me."

"Are all these birds from the country around here?"

"Mostly," the Doctor said. "A few rare ones visit me every year who would never come to England otherwise. But come, now I must show you the zoo."

# THE PRIVATE ZOO

I did not think there could be anything in the garden we had not seen. But then the Doctor took me by the arm to a small door in a high stone wall and pushed it open.

Inside was yet *another* garden! I expected to see cages with animals inside them like any other zoo. Instead, there were little stone houses, each with a window and door. As we walked in, many of the doors opened. Animals came running out to see us.

"Haven't the doors any locks on them?" I asked.

"Oh, yes, every door has a lock," he said. "But in my zoo, the doors open from the inside, not from the outside. The locks are there so the animals can have privacy whenever they want. Every animal in this zoo stays because he likes it."

"They all look very happy and clean. What are their names?"

The Doctor smiled. "That funny-looking thing with plates on his back, nosing under that brick, is a South American armadillo. The little chap talking to him is a Canadian woodchuck. They live in the holes at the foot of the wall. The two little beasts playing in the pond are Russian minks. . . . That reminds me, I must go and get them some herring before noon. That animal stepping out of his house is an antelope, and on the other side of the bushes I'll show you more."

"Are those deer over there?" I asked.

*"Deer?"* said the Doctor. "Where do you mean?"

"Over there. There are two of them," I said, pointing.

"Oh, that," said the Doctor, smiling. "That isn't two animals. It's one animal with two heads! It's the only two-headed animal in the world. It's called a pushmi-pullyu. I brought him from Africa. He's very tame. He's my night watchman for the zoo. He sleeps with one head at a time. The other head stays awake all night."

"Have you any lions or tigers?"

"No," said the Doctor. "It wouldn't be possible to keep them here, and I wouldn't even if I could! If I had my way, Stubbins, there wouldn't be a lion or tiger in a zoo in the world. They're never happy. They're always thinking of the big countries they left behind. You can see it in their eyes, dreaming of the big open spaces. And what are they given in exchange?" the Doctor asked, stopping in his walk and growing red with anger. "A bare cage with iron bars, an ugly piece of dead meat thrown at them once a day, and a crowd of fools who come to stare at them. No, Stubbins, lions and tigers should *never* be in zoos!"

The Doctor grew very serious, almost sad. Then, suddenly, he took me by the arm with his old cheerful smile. "We haven't seen the butterfly houses yet—nor the aquariums."

"Do butterflies have a language?"

"I'm sure they do," the Doctor said, "and the beetles, too. But so far I haven't learned much about insect languages. I've been so busy trying to master the shellfish."

Just then Polynesia flew up. "Doctor, there are two guinea pigs at the back door. They have run away from a boy who didn't give them the right food. They want to know if you'll take them in."

"All right," said the Doctor. "Show them the way to the zoo. Give them the house on the left, near the gate. Tell them the rules and give them a square meal. Now, Stubbins, we must go to the aquarium. I must show you the big glass seawater tank where I keep the shellfish."

# MY SCHOOLMASTER, POLYNESIA

After that, I was at the Doctor's house almost all day, every day. One evening my mother asked me jokingly why I did not take my bed over to the Doctor's house and live there.

I got to be quite useful to the Doctor, feeding his pets, helping to make new houses and fences for the zoo and helping with sick animals.

Polynesia came with me wherever I went, teaching me bird language and how to understand the animals' talking signs. It was hard. But the old parrot was patient with me, even though she sometimes had to work to keep her temper.

I began to understand the chatter of the birds and the talking antics of the dogs. I practiced listening to the mice at night after I went to bed.

The days passed, turning into weeks and months, and soon the roses in the garden lost their petals. Yellow leaves lay on the wide green lawn. Summer was nearly gone.

One day in the library Polynesia showed me some books about animals John Dolittle had written.

"What a lot of books the Doctor has! I wish I could read! It must be very interesting. Can you read, Polynesia?"

"Only a little," she said. "Be careful how you turn those pages—don't tear them. I don't really get enough time for much reading. That letter is a *k,* and this is a *b.*"

"What does this word under the picture mean?"

"Let me see," she said, and started to spell it out. "*B-A-B-O-O-N*—that's *monkey.* Reading isn't nearly as hard as it looks, once you know the letters."

"Polynesia," I said, "I want to ask you something very important."

"What is it, my boy?" she said.

"My mother doesn't think it's right that I come here for so many meals. Do you think if I did a whole lot more work for the Doctor I could come and live here? Instead of being paid like a regular gardener or workman, I would get my bed and meals for the work I did. What do you think?"

"You mean you want to be a proper assistant to the Doctor, is that it?"

"Yes, I guess so. You said yourself I could be useful to him."

"Well . . ." She thought a moment. "I really don't see why not. But is this what you want to be when you grow up, a naturalist?"

"Yes," I said. "I would sooner be a naturalist than anything else in the world."

"Let's go and speak to the Doctor about it," Polynesia said. "He's in the study."

# MY GREAT IDEA

The Doctor looked up and saw us at the door.

"Oh, come in, Stubbins," he said. "Did you wish to speak to me?"

"Doctor," I said. "I want to be a naturalist—like you—when I grow up."

"Oh, you do, do you?" murmured the Doctor. "Well! Have you spoken to your mother and father about it?"

"No, not yet," I said. "I want you to speak to them for me. Couldn't we make some plan so I could work for my meals and sleep here?"

The Doctor laughed. "You are quite welcome to come here for three meals a day all year round. You already do a lot of work. I've often felt I should pay you for what you do. But what was your plan?"

"Well," I said, "I thought perhaps you would see my mother and father. Tell them if they let me live here with you and work hard, that you will teach me to read and write. My mother is very anxious to have me learn reading and writing. And I couldn't be a proper naturalist without it, could I?"

"I don't know so much about that," said the Doctor. "It is nice to read and write. But the greatest naturalist of them all can't write his name or read the ABCs."

"Who is he?"

"A mysterious person," said the Doctor. "His name is Long Arrow, son of Golden Arrow. He is an Indian."

"Have you ever seen him?"

"No, I've never seen him," the Doctor said. "No European has ever met him. He lives with the animals and with different tribes of Indians somewhere along the mountains of Peru."

"How do you know so much about him if you've never seen him?"

"The purple bird of paradise," the Doctor said. "She told me about him. I gave her a message for him. I'm expecting her back any day now. But it is already the last week of August. I hope nothing happened to her on her way."

"Why do the animals and birds come to you when they are sick and not go to him?"

"It seems my methods are more up-to-date," the Doctor explained. "But Long Arrow's knowledge of natural history is tremendous. His specialty is botany—plants and that sort of thing. Now, Stubbins, are you sure you want to be a naturalist?"

"My mind is made up."

"It isn't a very good profession for making money. Most good naturalists don't *make* money, they *spend* it on butterfly nets and cases for birds' eggs and things. After all these years, I'm only now starting to make some money from the books I write."

"I don't care about money," I said. "Won't you please come and have dinner with my mother and father next Thursday? You see, there's another thing. If I'm living with you and sort of belong to your house and business, I could come with you on your next voyage!"

"Oh." He smiled. "So you want to come on a voyage with me?"

"I want to come on *all* your voyages. It would be much easier if you had someone to carry the butterfly nets and notebooks for you."

The Doctor sat, silently drumming his fingers on the desk, while I waited.

At last he stood up. "Well, Stubbins," he said, smiling. "I'll come and talk it over with you and your parents next Thursday. And . . . we'll see."

I tore home like the wind to tell my mother that the Doctor would come.

# A TRAVELER ARRIVES

The next day I sat talking to Dab-Dab on the Doctor's garden wall. Thanks to Polynesia's lessons, I could talk to most birds and some animals. Dab-Dab was a nice motherly duck, though not as clever and interesting as Polynesia. As we sat, Dab-Dab told me about her adventures in Africa with the Doctor long ago.

Suddenly we heard the sound of people cheering. I stood on the wall and saw a crowd of schoolchildren following a ragged, strange-looking woman.

"What can that be?" Dab-Dab cried.

The children laughed and shouted at the woman. She had long arms and stooped shoulders. She wore a straw hat on the side of her head. Her long skirt dragged on the ground. As she approached the wall, I saw that her hands were dark and hairy.

"Why, it's Chee-Chee!" Dab-Dab cried. "Come back at last! How dare they tease him!" She flew straight toward the children. They shrieked and raced back toward town.

*A traveler arrives.*

The strange-looking figure gazed after them, then climbed over the gate with ease. At last I saw the face under the hat. It was a monkey.

Chee-Chee dropped from the gate into the garden, ripped off the silly-looking clothes, tore the straw hat in two and threw it into the street. He pulled off his bodice and skirt and threw them down, angrily kicking them.

Suddenly there was a screech from the house, and out came Polynesia, followed by the Doctor and Jip.

"Chee-Chee! Chee-Chee!" shouted the parrot. "You've come at last! I told the Doctor you'd find a way! However did you do it?"

They gathered around, shaking Chee-Chee's four hands and asking a million questions at once. "Let's go into the house," the Doctor said. "Stubbins, would you run up to my bedroom? You'll find a bag of peanuts in the bureau drawer. I kept them in case Chee-Chee came back. And see if Dab-Dab has any bananas. Chee-Chee tells me he hasn't had one in two months!"

When I came into the kitchen, everyone was listening to the monkey tell of his journey from Africa.

# CHEE-CHEE'S VOYAGE

After Polynesia left Africa, Chee-Chee grew homesick for Doctor Dolittle and Puddleby. One day, down at the seashore, he saw people getting on a ship going to England. He tried to get on too but was turned away.

He watched as the people boarded, and saw a large family getting on the ship. One of the girls reminded him of his cousin. *That girl looks just as much like a monkey as I look like a girl,* he thought. *If I could get some clothes to wear, I could slip onto the ship with another family.*

He went off to a nearby house and looked through the open window. He knew it was wrong, but he jumped through the window, grabbed some clothes and put them on. He went back to the shore, moved among the crowds and sneaked safely onto the big ship.

When he reached England, the sailors saw him as he tried to get off the ship. They wanted to keep him as a pet. He dived into the crowd and escaped. He was still a long distance from Puddleby and had to travel across all of England.

He hid during the day and came out at night to look for food. Chee-Chee sighed, recalling the terrible time. Whenever he passed through a town, crowds of children ran after him, laughing. Sometimes people caught him and tried to stop him, forcing him to run up lampposts to escape. He slept anywhere he could hide and lived on berries and cobnuts. After many adventures and narrow escapes, he spotted the tower of Puddleby Church. He knew that at last he was near home.

When Chee-Chee finished his story, he ate six bananas and drank a bowl of milk.

"Why wasn't I born with wings like Polynesia, so I could fly here?" he asked the Doctor. "How I hated that hat and skirt! Why on earth do women wear them? I was so glad to see old Puddleby this morning!"

"Your bed on top of the plate rack in the scullery is all ready for you," said the Doctor. "We left it, in case you might come back."

"Thanks," Chee-Chee said. "It's good to be back in the old house again. Well, I think I'll go to bed now. I need sleep."

Chee-Chee climbed the plate rack the way a sailor climbs a mast. He curled himself up on the top and within a minute was snoring peacefully.

"Good old Chee-Chee," the Doctor whispered. "I'm glad he's back."

"Yes, good old Chee-Chee!" echoed Dab-Dab and Polynesia as we all tiptoed out of the scullery and closed the door.

# I BECOME A DOCTOR'S ASSISTANT

Thursday evening there was great excitement at our house. My mother prepared all the Doctor's favorite dishes: spareribs, sliced beets, fried bread, shrimps and treacle tart. She fussed around the house to see if everything was tidy.

At last we heard a knock on the door.

The Doctor had brought his own flute with him this time.

After supper the table was cleared away. The Doctor and my father started playing duets. They were so interested in the music, I was afraid they would forget about my business. At last the Doctor said, "Your son tells me he is anxious to become a naturalist."

That began a long talk that lasted far into the night. My mother and father were against the idea. They called it silly and said I would get tired of it.

Then the Doctor turned to my father. "Supposing, Mr. Stubbins, your son came to me for two years—until he is twelve years old. He will have time to see if he grows tired of it. During that time, I promise to teach him reading, writing and perhaps a little arithmetic. What about that?"

"I don't know," my father said, shaking his head. "Tommy ought to be learning a trade so he can earn a living later on."

Suddenly my mother spoke up. "Now, Jacob," she said to my father. "You know that many lads in the town have been in grammar school till they were fourteen or fifteen. Tommy can easily spare two years for education. If he learns no more than to read and write, the time will not be lost. Though goodness knows," she said, sniffing into her handkerchief, "the house will seem terribly empty when he's gone."

"I will take care that he comes to see you every day if you like, Mrs. Stubbins," said Doctor Dolittle.

Finally my father gave in. It was agreed that I would live with the Doctor and work for him in exchange for learning to read and write and for my board and lodging.

I whispered in the Doctor's ear, "Please don't forget to say something about the voyages."

"Oh, by the way," John Dolittle said at once. "Occasionally my work requires me to travel. You will have no objections to your son's coming with me to help?"

I stood behind the Doctor's chair, my heart thumping with excitement, waiting for my father's answer.

"No," he said slowly, after a while. "If we agree to the other arrangement, I don't see how we can object to that."

There was never a happier boy in the world than I was at that moment. I knew it was almost time for the Doctor to start on another voyage. Polynesia told me he never stayed home for more than six months. He would surely be going again in just a few weeks. And I, Tommy Stubbins, would go with him—to cross the sea, to walk on foreign shores, to roam the world!

# Part II

# THE CREW OF THE *CURLEW*

Two days after dinner at my family's house, the Doctor told me sadly he would have to give up learning the language of shellfish at present.

"I'm discouraged, Stubbins. I've tried the mussels, clams, oysters, all the lobster and crab family. I think I'll go back to it later," he said.

"What will you do now?" I asked.

"Well, I think it's time for a voyage," he said.

"When shall we start?"

"We'll have to wait for the purple bird of paradise. She might have a message from Long Arrow. She should have been here ten days ago!"

"Shouldn't we see about a boat?" I said. "She'll probably be here any day and we'll have lots to do."

"That's true," said the Doctor. "Let's go see Joe, the mussel man. Maybe he knows of a boat for us."

So off we went, Jip tagging along with us. Joe, the mussel man, took us a little way down the river. There was the prettiest vessel ever built. She was called the *Curlew*. Joe said he would sell her cheap but we had to have three people to sail her.

"Of course there'll be Chee-Chee," the Doctor said. "But although he is quick he is not as strong as a man. We do need another person to sail a boat as big as that."

"I know a first-class seaman who could use a job," Joe said.

"No thanks," said the Doctor. "I couldn't afford a seaman. Who else could we take with us?"

"There's Matthew Mugg, the cat's-meat man," I said.

"No. Matthew's a nice fellow, but he talks too much. You must be very careful whom you take on long voyages."

"How about Luke the Hermit?" I asked.

"Splendid idea, Stubbins!" the Doctor smiled. "Let's ask him right away."

# LUKE THE HERMIT

The Hermit was a peculiar old friend of ours. He lived alone far out in the marshes in a little shack with his brindle bulldog, Bob. He never saw or talked to people. If they came near his hut, Bob drove them away. Everyone in Puddleby referred to him as Luke the Hermit and said there was some mystery about him. But no one seemed to know what it was.

Only the Doctor and I ever visited with Luke. Bob never barked when he heard us coming. We liked Luke, and he liked us.

As we crossed the marshes to the little shack, a cold wind blew eastward. Jip put up his ears as we neared the cabin.

"That's funny," he said.

"What is it?" asked the Doctor.

"Bob hasn't come out to meet us. He should have heard or smelled us coming. And what's that noise?"

"Sounds like a gate creaking," the Doctor said.

We hurried along anxiously.

When we reached the shack, the door was wide open, creaking in the wind. There was no one inside.

"Perhaps Luke is out for a walk?" I said.

"He is *always* home." The Doctor frowned. "Even if he *did* go out for a walk, he wouldn't leave the door open like this." He looked in as Jip sniffed around. "What is it, Jip?" he asked.

"Nothing worth speaking of," the dog said, examining the floor carefully.

"Come here, Jip," the Doctor said sternly. "You are hiding something, or see signs of something. What has happened? Tell me."

"I don't know," Jip said guiltily.

"I can tell from the look in your eye that you know something," the Doctor said. "What is it?"

Jip didn't answer.

The Doctor questioned him for ten minutes. The dog did not say a word.

"There's no use standing here in the cold," the Doctor said finally. "Let's get home to lunch. The Hermit's gone."

We started back across the marsh. Jip dashed ahead of us, pretending to chase water rats.

"He knows something," whispered the Doctor.

"You think he knows about the mystery of the Hermit?" I asked.

"I shouldn't wonder if he did," the Doctor answered slowly. "There was something in his face the minute we got there and the door was open. The way he sniffed the floor—that told him something. He saw signs we couldn't. I'll ask him again. Here, Jip! Jip, where are you?"

"Jip!" I called. "Jip . . . Jip . . . Jip . . . *Jip!*"

But he was gone. We called and called. We even walked back to the hut. Jip had disappeared.

"He must have run ahead of us to home," I said to the Doctor, who shook his head.

"Odd," he muttered. "Very odd."

## The Third Chapter

# JIP AND THE SECRET

The first thing the Doctor asked Dab-Dab when we reached home was, "Is Jip here yet?"

"No, I haven't seen him," Dab-Dab said.

"Please let me know the moment he comes in," the Doctor said as he hung up his hat.

"Don't be long washing up," Dab-Dab said. "Lunch is on the table."

Just as we sat down to lunch in the kitchen, we heard a racket at the front door. I ran to open it. In bounded Jip.

"Doctor!" he cried. "Come to the library, quick! Just you and Tommy."

Inside the library, with the door closed, Jip asked the Doctor to lock it with a key. "And make sure no one is listening at the windows."

"It's all right," said the Doctor. "Now, what is it?"

"Well, Doctor," said Jip, gasping from running. "I know all about the Hermit. I have for years. But I couldn't tell you because I swore to Bob that I would keep the secret."

"Are you going to tell me now?"

"Yes," said Jip. "We've got to save him. I followed Bob's scent when I left you in the marshes. I found him and asked if I could tell you now. Maybe you can do something!"

"Well, for heaven's sake go on!" the Doctor nearly shouted. "What is the mystery? What has happened? Where is the Hermit?"

"He's in Puddleby Jail!" Jip said.

"In prison!"

"Yes."

"What's he done?"

Jip went to the door and smelled the bottom to see if anyone was listening. He walked back to the Doctor and whispered, *"He killed a man!"*

"Lord preserve us!" the Doctor said, falling into a chair and wiping his brow with a handkerchief. "When did he do it?"

"Fifteen years ago in a Mexican gold mine. That's why he's been a hermit ever since. He shaved his beard and kept people away, living alone with Bob on the marshes so he wouldn't be recognized. Last week, these policemen came to town. They heard that a strange man lived alone in the shack and got suspicious. People had been hunting all over the world for the man who did that killing. The policemen went to the shack and recognized Luke by a mole on his arm. Took him straight to prison."

"Who would have thought it! Luke the philosopher," the Doctor murmured. "Killed a man. I can't believe it."

"Unfortunately, it's true," Jip said. "But it wasn't his fault. Bob says so. He was there and saw it all. He was scarcely more than a puppy. Bob says Luke couldn't help it. He *had* to do it."

"Where is Bob now?" the Doctor asked.

"He's at the prison. I wanted him to come see you, but he won't leave the prison while Luke's there. Please come down there, Doctor, and see what you can do. The trial is at two o'clock this afternoon. What time is it now?"

"Ten past one!"

"Bob says they'll kill Luke for punishment if they can prove he did it, or at least send him to prison for the rest of his life."

"Of course I'll come," said the Doctor, getting up to go. "But I'm afraid there is not much I can do to help. And yet . . ." His face turned thoughtful. "I wonder. . . ."

Then he opened the door and headed out, with Jip and me following.

## The Fourth Chapter

# BOB

As we hurried out the door, Dab-Dab gave us some pork pies wrapped up to eat on the way for lunch. When we got to Puddleby Courthouse, next door to the prison, a huge crowd surrounded the building.

I hung on to the Doctor's coattails as he marched through the mob and safely into the jail.

"I want to see Luke," he said to a guard standing at the door.

Outside the door of Luke's cell, Bob, the bulldog, wagged his tail sadly when he saw us.

At first I couldn't see anything, it was so dark. After a while I saw a low bed against the wall, under a small window with bars. On the bed sat the Hermit, staring at the floor, his head resting on his hands.

*On the bed sat the Hermit.*

"Well, Luke," the Doctor said. "They don't give you much light in here!"

Very slowly the Hermit looked up. "John Dolittle. What brings you here?"

"I've come to see you. I only just heard about it or I would have come sooner. I went to your hut to ask if you'd join me on a voyage. I've come to see if there is anything I can do."

"Thanks, but I don't imagine anything can be done. They've caught me at last. That's it, I suppose." He got up stiffly and paced around the little room.

"In a way, I'm glad it's over," he said. "I never had any peace, thinking they were after me. Afraid to speak to anyone."

The Doctor talked to Luke for more than half an hour, trying to cheer him. Then he said he wanted to see Bob. We knocked on the door and were led out of Luke's cell by the policeman.

"Bob," the Doctor called to the bulldog. "Come with me to the porch. I want to ask you something."

We walked down the corridor, and the Doctor continued, "Now, tell me, Bob: You saw this business happen, didn't you? You were there when the man was killed, eh?"

"I was, Doctor," Bob said, "and I tell you—"

"All right," the Doctor interrupted. "That's all I want to know for now. There isn't time for more. The trial is about to begin. Now, listen, Bob. I want you to stay with me in the courtroom. And whatever I tell you to do, do it. Don't make any scenes. Don't bite or growl, no matter what they say about Luke. Just behave quietly and answer any question I may ask you. Tell the truth. Do you understand?"

"Very well. But do you think you'll be able to get him off, Doctor?" asked Bob.

"We'll see, Bob. I'm going to try a new thing. I'm not sure the judge will allow it. Now we must go into the courtroom. Remember: Don't bite anyone or you'll spoil everything."

# MENDOZA

The courtroom was very solemn. It was a big, high room. The judge was seated at his desk. He was an old, handsome man in a black robe and big wig of gray hair. Below him at another desk sat lawyers in white wigs.

The Doctor tapped me and whispered, "See those twelve men at the side. That's the jury. They decide whether or not Luke is guilty."

"Look!" I said, pointing. "There's Luke."

"I'm going to speak to one of those men in white wigs," the Doctor said. "Wait here and keep these two seats for us. Keep Bob with you. Hold on to his collar." The Doctor disappeared into the crowded main part of the room.

I saw the judge pick up a wooden hammer and knock on his desk. Everyone stopped talking and turned to him. Then another man in a black gown stood up and read from a paper in his hand.

Suddenly the Doctor was behind me with one of the men in white wigs. He introduced him as Mr. Percy Jenkyns, Luke's lawyer, and said it was his job to get Luke off, if he could. We shook hands.

"Oh, I think it is a perfectly precious idea," the lawyer said. "Of *course* the dog must be admitted as a witness! He was the only one who saw the thing take place. This will stir things. A bulldog witness for defense! I do hope there are reporters present. I shall be known after this! And won't Conkey be pleased?" His eyes twinkled.

"Who is Conkey?" I asked the Doctor.

"Conkey is the judge, the Honorable Eustace Beauchamp Conckley."

The trial began, and people kept going to the place the Doctor called the witness box. The lawyers asked questions "about the night of the twenty-ninth." Then the people would get down from the witness box and others would take their place.

One of the lawyers (who the Doctor later told me was called the prosecutor) was a nasty-looking man. He tried to make the Hermit look as if he had always been a bad man.

But most of the time, I could not keep my eyes off Luke, who stared at the floor. He didn't show any interest until a small, dark man with wicked, watery eyes went to the witness box. Bob snarled under my chair when this man came into the courtroom. Luke's eyes blazed angrily.

The man said his name was Mendoza. He had brought the police to the mine after the man, whose name was Bluebeard Bill, had been killed. After every word Mendoza spoke, I could hear Bob muttering. Both the Doctor and I had hard work keeping Bob under the seat.

Next Mr. Jenkyns stood before the judge. "Your Honor, I wish to introduce a new witness for the defense, Doctor John Dolittle, the naturalist. Please step into the witness box, Doctor."

Excitement buzzed through the courtroom as the Doctor walked to the front.

Mr. Jenkyns asked the Doctor questions about himself. He made him answer in a loud voice so the whole courtroom could hear. "Are you prepared to swear, Doctor Dolittle, that you understand the language of dogs and can make them understand you?"

"Yes, that is so," the Doctor said.

"And what, might I ask," said the judge in a quiet, dignified voice, "has any of this to do with the killing of, er, er . . . Bluebeard Bill?"

"Your Honor," Mr. Jenkyns said, talking in a very grand manner. "There is in this courtroom a bulldog who was the only living thing to see the man killed. With the court's permission I would like to put that dog on the witness stand and have him questioned by Doctor John Dolittle!"

# THE JUDGE'S DOG

At first there was silence in the court. Then everyone began whispering and giggling.

"I protest, Your Honor!" the nasty lawyer cried, wildly waving his arms in front of the judge.

Mr. Jenkyns stood up again. "Your Honor will have no objection, I hope, to a demonstration by the Doctor of his powers—to prove that he can understand the speech of animals?"

A twinkle came into the old judge's eyes. He sat for a moment before answering.

"No, I don't think so," he said, turning to the Doctor. "Are you quite sure you can do this?"

"Quite, Your Honor," said the Doctor.

"Very well then," said the judge. "If you can satisfy us that you really are able to understand canine testimony, the dog shall be admitted as a witness."

"I protest, I protest!" yelled the prosecutor.

"Sit down!" the judge yelled.

"What animal does Your Honor wish me to talk with?" asked the Doctor.

"I would like you to talk to my own dog," said the judge. "Bring him in," he ordered the guard.

Moments later, a great Russian wolfhound with slender legs and a shaggy coat was led into the courtroom.

"Now, Doctor," asked the judge. "Did you ever see this dog before?"

"No, Your Honor. I never saw him before."

"Fine. Will you please ask him what I had for supper last night? He was with me and watched while I ate."

The Doctor and the dog started talking in signs and sounds. The Doctor began to giggle and seemed to forget about the court, judge and jury.

"Have you finished yet?" the judge asked. "It shouldn't take that long just to ask what I had for supper."

"Oh, no, Your Honor, but then he went on to tell what you did after supper."

"Never mind that," said the judge. "What answer did he give you to my question?"

"He said you had a mutton chop, two baked potatoes, a pickled walnut, and a glass of ale."

The Honorable Eustace Beauchamp Conckley turned pale.

"Sounds like witchcraft," he muttered. "I never dreamed—"

"And after your supper," the Doctor went on, "he said you went to a prizefight and then sat up playing cards until midnight—"

"That will do," the judge interrupted. "I am satisfied you can do as you say. The prisoner's dog shall be admitted as a witness."

"I protest! I protest!" screamed the prosecutor. "Your Honor—"

"Sit down and shut up!" roared the judge. "I say the dog shall be heard. Put the witness on the stand."

And for the first time in the history of England, a dog was put in the witness stand of Her Majesty's Court. And I, Tommy Stubbins, proudly led Bob up the aisle on a signal from the Doctor. We walked through the astonished crowd, past the frowning, spluttering prosecutor to the witness box, where the old bulldog sat scowling over the rail at the amazed jury.

*The old bulldog sat scowling over
the rail at the amazed jury.*

## The Seventh Chapter

# THE END OF THE MYSTERY

The trial went quickly forward after that. Mr. Jenkyns told the Doctor to ask Bob what he had seen on the night of the twenty-ninth. Bob told all he knew, and the Doctor turned it into English for the judge and jury.

He said that on November 29, 1824, he was with his master, Luke, and his partners, Manuel Mendoza and William Boggs, also known as Bluebeard Bill. The three were searching for gold, which they discovered on the morning of the twenty-ninth. They were all very happy. Bob was suspicious of Mendoza and followed him when he asked Bluebeard Bill to go for a walk. Bob heard them arrange to kill Luke so they could get the gold and share it.

At this point the judge asked, "Where is the witness Mendoza? Constable, see that he does not leave the court." But Mendoza had already sneaked out and was never seen in Puddleby again.

Bob went on to tell how he tried to warn Luke, but Luke didn't understand dog language. So Bob decided not to let him out of sight, and stayed with him every moment of the day and night.

The hole where they had found the gold was so deep that a huge bucket was used to haul the men up and down to dig. That night, Luke was hauling up Bluebeard Bill. When Mendoza saw this, he thought Luke was stealing the gold. He drew a pistol and came sneaking up behind Luke.

Bob tried to warn Luke, but Luke took no notice of him. So Bob bit his master in the leg from behind. Luke was so startled that he let go of the rope and then—*crash!* —down went Bill to the bottom of the mine and was killed.

Mendoza said that Luke had killed Bluebeard Bill and he was going to get the police. Mendoza hoped to get the whole mine for himself.

Luke was afraid. If Mendoza told enough lies, it *would* look as if he had killed Bill on purpose. While Mendoza was gone, Luke and Bob stole away and came to England, where they had been in hiding ever since.

When the Doctor had finished translating Bob's testimony, the excitement among the jury was incredible. The prosecutor waved his arms more wildly than ever.

*He drew a pistol and came sneaking up.*

"Your Honor, I object that this evidence is biased. Of course the dog would not testify against his own master!"

"Very well, you may cross-examine. It is your duty as prosecutor to prove his evidence untrue."

The lawyer looked as if he would have a fit. He opened his mouth, but no words came out. Clutching his forehead, he sank into his seat. He was half carried from the courtroom muttering, "I protest. I object. I protest!"

# THREE CHEERS

The judge made a long speech to the jury about the law. Then the twelve jury members went into the next room. The Doctor came back to his seat, leading Bob.

We waited a short time, and then the courtroom fell silent as the jury members filed back to their seats. The leader of the jury stood up and turned to the judge.

"Your Honor," the man said, "the jury returns a verdict of *Not Guilty.*"

"What does that mean?" I asked the Doctor, who was standing on top of his chair, dancing like a schoolboy.

"It means he's free!" he cried. "Luke is free!"

The whole courtroom went wild. But the celebration stopped suddenly as the judge stood up and walked from the courtroom. The people stood respectfully and quietly. The trial of Luke the Hermit was over.

In the hush as the judge was leaving, a shriek rang out from a woman at the door. "Luke! I've found you at last!"

"It's his wife," a woman in front of me whispered. "Hasn't seen 'im in fifteen years, poor dear! What a lovely reunion."

"Come on, Stubbins," said the Doctor, taking me by the arm, "let's get out of this while we can."

"Are you going to speak to Luke, to ask him to come on the voyage?" I asked.

"It would be of no use," said the Doctor. "His wife's come for him after fifteen years. Let's get home to tea!"

As we stepped out the side door, the crowd shouted, "The Doctor! The Doctor! The Hermit would have hanged without the Doctor! Speech!"

"The people are calling for you, sir," said a man, running up after us.

"I'm so sorry, I'm in a big hurry," the Doctor said politely. "I have an appointment at my house. Tell Luke to make a speech." He grabbed my hand, and we walked briskly away.

"Oh, Lord," he muttered as we got into the open air. "Another crowd! Run up the alleyway, Stubbins!" We darted through some side streets and ran until we reached the Oxenthorpe Road. In the distance we could still hear the crowd. "Three cheers for Luke the Hermit: Hooray!—Three cheers for his dog: Hooray!—Three cheers for his wife: Hooray!—Three cheers for Doctor Dolittle: Hooray! Hooray! *Hoo-ray!*"

# THE PURPLE BIRD OF PARADISE

Polynesia was waiting on the front porch.

"Doctor," she said. "The purple bird of paradise has arrived!"

"At last!" he sighed. "How is Miranda?" He fumbled excitedly for his keys.

"She seemed all right when she arrived, though exhausted from her long journey," Polynesia said. "But that mischief-making sparrow, Cheapside, insulted her as soon as she came into the garden, and she broke down in tears. She was ready to go back to Brazil! I had the hardest time making her stay. She's in the study. I shut Cheapside in one of your bookcases."

The Doctor frowned and walked quickly to the study. Dab-Dab stood guarding the glass-fronted bookcases where Cheapside was held. The noisy sparrow fluttered angrily behind the glass.

In the center of the big table, perched on the ink-stand, stood the most beautiful bird I have ever seen. She had a deep violet-colored breast, scarlet wings and a long, sweeping tail of gold. She was incredibly beautiful but looked very tired. Her head was under her wing. She swayed gently from side to side like a bird that has flown long and far.

"Shhh!" Dab-Dab whispered. "Miranda is asleep. Send Cheapside away before he does more harm. Would you like tea here or in the kitchen?"

"We'll come into the kitchen when we're ready, thank you," the Doctor said. "Let Cheapside out before you go, please." Dab-Dab opened the bookcase. Cheapside strutted out, trying hard not to look guilty.

"Cheapside, what did you say to Miranda?" the Doctor demanded.

"Nothing, Doc, I swear I didn't. Nothing much, anyhow. She comes swanking into the garden, turning up her nose, just because she has lots of colored plumage. I don't hold with those gaudy foreigners. A London sparrow's just as good. I only said, 'You don't belong in an English garden, you should be in a milliner's window.'"

"You should be ashamed of yourself, Cheapside. This bird has come thousands of miles only to be insulted by your nasty tongue in my garden? If she had gone before I returned I would never have forgiven you. Leave the room, now."

Trying to look as if he didn't care, the sparrow hopped out the door, and Dab-Dab closed it behind him. The Doctor went up to the beautiful bird and gently stroked her back. Instantly her head popped out from under her wing.

# LONG ARROW, THE SON OF GOLDEN ARROW

"Miranda, my dear, I'm so sorry this happened," said the Doctor.

Miranda stretched her gorgeous wings wearily. There were tears in her eyes, and her beak was trembling.

"I wouldn't have minded so much," she said in a high voice, "if I hadn't been so dreadfully worn out. That and something else," she sighed.

"Did you have a hard trip?" the Doctor asked.

"The worst passage I ever made. The weather . . . don't ask. Anyhow, I'm here," she said.

"Tell me," said the Doctor. "What did Long Arrow say when you gave him my message?"

"That's the worst part of it!" Miranda said. "I couldn't deliver your message or find Long Arrow. *He's disappeared!*"

"Disappeared!" the Doctor cried in disbelief. "What could have happened to him?"

"Nobody knows," Miranda said. "The Indians didn't know where he was. That's why I'm so late in coming to you. I kept hunting and hunting, went the whole length and breadth of South America! There wasn't a living thing that could tell me where he was."

A sad silence filled the room. The Doctor frowned. Polynesia scratched her head. "Did you ask the black parrots?" she asked.

"Certainly!" Miranda said. "I was so upset at not finding any news, I forgot about observing the weather signs before I left. I ran into a wild storm in the mid-Atlantic. Luckily I found a piece of wrecked vessel and roosted on it after the storm died down. If I hadn't taken that rest I wouldn't have made it here."

"Poor Miranda!" said the Doctor. "Do you know where Long Arrow was last seen?"

"A young albatross said he'd seen him on Spider Monkey Island."

"That's somewhere off the coast of Brazil, isn't it?" the Doctor asked.

"Yes," Miranda said. "I flew there and asked every bird on the whole island. Long Arrow was visiting some

*"What else can I think?"*

Indians there and was last seen going into the mountains looking for rare medicinal plants."

"Do you think some accident befell him?" the Doctor asked fearfully.

"I'm afraid it must have," Miranda said, shaking her head.

"It would be the greatest disappointment in my life if I could never meet Long Arrow," the Doctor confessed. "He knew more natural science than all of us put together. If he has gone without someone to write it down for him, it would be a terrible loss. But you don't really think he is dead, do you?" he asked hopefully.

"What else can I think," asked Miranda, bursting into tears, "when he has not been seen by flesh, fish or fowl for six whole months?"

# BLIND TRAVEL

Everyone was sad about the news of Long Arrow, but the Doctor was the most upset. He took his tea silently, staring at spots on the tablecloth as though his thoughts were far away.

I tried to cheer him by reminding him of the good he had done that day for Luke and his wife. When that didn't help, I talked about our plans for the voyage.

"But you see, Stubbins," the Doctor said, "I don't know where to go now. I planned this voyage specifically to see Long Arrow. I thought perhaps he could help me with the language of the shellfish and find a way to get to the bottom of the sea." He sat silently. "Although Long Arrow and I never met, I felt I knew him well."

We went back into the study, where the Doctor put on his robe and lit his pipe. "But we'll still go on a voyage, won't we?" I asked. "Even if you can't find Long Arrow?"

He looked sharply into my face, then smiled suddenly when he saw how anxious I was.

"Yes, Stubbins, don't worry. We can't stop working and learning. The question is: Where to go?"

Suddenly the Doctor sat up. "We'll play Blind Travel," he said. "It's a game I used to play when I couldn't make up my mind where to go on a voyage. You open an atlas to a page, wave a pencil and touch it down. Wherever it touches you are sworn to go. Want to play?"

"Oh, yes!" I said excitedly.

"Good! Take the pencil, and stand close to the table. When the book falls open, wave the pencil around three times and jab it down. Now, shut your eyes."

It was a tense and fearful moment. We both shut our eyes tightly. I heard the book fall open. I waved the pencil three times in a circle and lowered my hand.

The pencil touched down on the page. "It's done," I said.

*It was a tense and fearful moment.*

# Destiny and Destination

e opened our eyes. The atlas was opened to a map called "Chart of the South Atlantic Ocean." The Doctor needed his glasses to read the small print where the pencil point rested.

"'Spider Monkey Island,'" he read slowly. He whistled softly under his breath. "How extraordinary! You've hit upon the last place Long Arrow was seen alive. Well, well!"

"We'll go there, Doctor, won't we?" I asked.

"Of course we will. With a good boat and good wind we could easily make it in four weeks. Of all the places in the world . . . Spider Monkey Island! At last I will be able to get some jabizri beetles. There are only three countries in the world where they are found, and Spider Monkey Island is one of them."

"What does the little question mark after the name mean?" I asked.

"It means that the island's position in the ocean is not exactly known. We might be the first people to land there. We also might have trouble finding it. But that's what a voyage is about!"

"Will there be natives there?" I asked.

The Doctor nodded. "Miranda tells me a peculiar tribe of Indians lives there." Suddenly the sleeping bird of paradise awoke. In our excitement, we had forgotten to whisper.

"We're going to Spider Monkey Island, Miranda," the Doctor said. "You know where it is, don't you?"

"I know where it was," she said. "I don't know if it will be in the same place, though. Didn't you know that it is a *floating* island? It moves all over the place, usually near southern South America. I could find it for you, if you want to go there."

I was so excited, I bolted from the room to find Chee-Chee and share the news. At the door I bumped into Dab-Dab and started dancing around.

"Where do you think you're going?" cried the duck.

"To Spider Monkey Island!" I shouted, doing cartwheels down the hall. "A *floating* island!"

# Part III

# THE THIRD MAN

**W**e began preparing for the voyage immediately. Joe, the mussel man, had the *Curlew* tied near the river wall to make it easier to load. We spent three days filling the boat with supplies. The boat had three little cabins, a saloon (or dining room) and, under all this, a hold, where the food, extra sails and other things were kept.

Everyone in town must have heard about our voyage because there were always crowds watching as we put things on board. Matthew Mugg was among them.

"Where is the Doctor going this time, Tommy?" he asked.

"Spider Monkey Island," I said proudly.

"Are you the only one going with him?" Matthew asked.

"He said he'd like to take another man but hasn't made up his mind," I explained.

A big man with a red beard and tattoos on his arms stopped me as I was loading. "Boy," he called, "where's the skipper?"

"The skipper? Oh, you mean the Doctor. He's not here yet," I said.

Just then the Doctor came in sight, loaded down with notebooks and butterfly nets. The man went up to him.

"Morning, Captain," he said. "Heard you needed hands for a voyage. I'm Ben Butcher, able seaman."

"Very glad to know you," the Doctor said, "but I can't take on any more hands, thanks anyhow."

"But, Captain, surely you ain't going to face deep-sea weather with nothing more than this bit of a lad, and on a ship this big!" he said.

The Doctor was polite but firm. Finally the man walked away, muttering that we'd never make it alive back to land.

Just as soon as the Doctor went below, a distinguished-looking man, fashionably dressed, came onto the gangplank.

"Pardon me," he said, bowing elegantly. "Is this the ship of the physician Dolittle?"

"Yes," I said. "Did you wish to see him?"

"I did—if it is not discommodious," he answered. "I am Bumpo Kahbooboo, Crown Prince of Jolliginki."

*"Boy, where's the skipper?"*

I ran down and told the Doctor. "How fortunate!" he cried. "My old friend Bumpo. I heard he was studying at Oxford. How good of him to call on me!"

Prince Bumpo was overjoyed to see the Doctor and shook his hand warmly.

"News reached me of your voyage," the Prince said. "I am sublimely ecstasied that I did not miss you!"

"You very nearly did. We were waiting to get another man to help sail the boat."

"I detect something of the finger of Destination in this," Bumpo said. "How would *I* do?"

"Splendidly! But what about your studies?" the Doctor asked.

"I need a holiday," said Bumpo. "And traveling with you would not neglect my edification, that I know." He smiled. "Before I left Jolliginki, my august father, the King, told me to be sure and travel."

"Well, Bumpo, if you are sure you want to come, we'd love to have you. I think you are exactly the man we need."

# GOODBYE!

Two days later we were ready to set sail. Jip begged so hard to come that the Doctor finally agreed. Polynesia and Chee-Chee were the only other animals to go with us. Dab-Dab was in charge of the house and the animal family left behind.

Down at the river wall, a great crowd gathered to see us off. My mother and father were at the gangplank. I hoped they would not make a scene, but they behaved quite well—for parents.

We were surprised not to see Matthew Mugg. The Doctor wanted to give him instructions about food for the animals at home. At last we got the anchor up, and the *Curlew* moved gently down the river with the tide. The crowd on the wall cheered, waving handkerchiefs.

It was an incredible feeling, getting into the open sea as we passed the lighthouse at the mouth of the river. It was so new and different.

I looked around and took a deep breath. The Doctor steered the boat as it leaped and plunged gently through the waves. Bumpo was downstairs preparing dinner. Chee-Chee coiled up ropes in the stern and laid them in neat piles. My job was to fasten things down on the deck so nothing would roll about if the weather got rough. Jip was at the peak of the boat, sitting like a statue, ears cocked and nose stuck out, keeping a lookout for wrecks, sandbars and other dangers. Everyone had a job to do. Even Polynesia took the sea's temperature to make sure there were no icebergs nearby. I realized the voyage had really begun. It would soon be my first night at sea!

# OUR TROUBLES BEGIN

Just before supper, Bumpo went to the Doctor at the wheel to report a stowaway in the hold.

"What a nuisance," said the Doctor. "Stubbins, go with Bumpo and bring the man up."

Bumpo and I went into the hold. Hiding behind the flour bags we found Matthew Mugg! We hauled him upstairs to the Doctor.

"Matthew, what on earth are you doing here?" John Dolittle said.

"The temptation was too much for me, Doc. You know I always wanted to go on a voyage. And when I heard you needed a man, I thought if I hid till the ship was at sea, you'd keep me. But this ship rolls so! How long has this storm been going on?"

"Matthew, you shouldn't have come," the Doctor said. "We'll stop in Penzance and put you ashore. You will take the coach from Penzance to Bristol, and then it's not far to Puddleby. Don't forget to take the usual food to the animals in the house every Thursday. And don't forget the extra herring for the minks."

Chee-Chee and I set about lighting the lamps. We put a green light on the right side, a red one on the left and a white one on the mast.

We all turned at the sound of people coming up to the deck. "Bumpo, what's this!" cried John Dolittle.

"Two more stowaways, sir, hiding under the bunk in your cabin. One woman and one man, sir," he said.

"Who are they?" the Doctor asked. "I can't see their faces in this dim light."

It was Luke and his wife. Mrs. Luke was very seasick. Luke explained that after the trial so many people had come to see them in their shack in the marsh that life had become impossible. They decided to escape from Puddleby but had no money to go any way other than on the Doctor's ship. Luke apologized many times for the inconvenience. The Doctor said he would give them some money and a letter to a man he knew in Penzance who, he hoped, would be able to find some work for Luke.

Polynesia was sitting on my shoulder as we watched, muttering. "There he goes, giving away all the money we've got. What if we run out of food? Now we haven't the price of a postage stamp!"

With the help of the map, a compass and the lighthouses, the Doctor steered the ship into port without hitting a rock or a sandbar. He took the stowaways to shore in our small rowboat and found them rooms at the hotel. By then it was after midnight. We decided to stay in the harbor until the morning. I was glad to get to bed. Rocked by the sea, I was asleep in minutes.

# OUR TROUBLES CONTINUE

The next morning, while eating an excellent breakfast of kidneys and bacon, the Doctor asked if I thought we should stop at the Capa Blanca Islands or head straight to Brazil.

I reminded him that Miranda said we had about four weeks of good weather and should probably go straight to Brazil. "She'll be looking for us and will wonder what happened if we're not there in a month," I said.

"Quite true," John Dolittle said. "But the Capa Blancas make a convenient stopping place if we need supplies or repairs. They're about six days away. Well, we'll see how it goes."

We left Penzance Harbor, and everything went smoothly for several days.

I grew fond of our funny friend Bumpo, with his grand way of speaking. Someone was always falling over his huge feet. He kept everyone in good humor.

On the fifth day out, Bumpo came up from the kitchen. "The salt beef is nearly all gone," he told the Doctor.

"But we brought a hundred and twenty pounds. We couldn't have eaten that in five days!" the Doctor cried.

"I don't know," Bumpo said. "But if it's rats, they are awfully fat rodents!"

"We must search the hold," Polynesia said. "Come with me, Tommy."

We went quietly into the storeroom. Soon we heard snoring coming from the corner of the hold.

"I thought so," Polynesia said. "It's a man. Haul him out. We seem to have brought all of Puddleby with us."

It was Ben Butcher, able seaman. Polynesia sputtered like a firecracker. "This is the last straw!" she said. "Bring him up to the Doctor."

We led the huge man to the wheel, where he greeted the Doctor.

"Another stowaway, sir," Bumpo reported.

This time, I thought the Doctor would throw a fit.

"Ben Butcher, able seaman, at your service," the man said to the Doctor. "I knew you'd need me, so I took the liberty of stowing away. I'll soon have things shipshape."

"I told you in Puddleby I didn't want you to come!" roared the Doctor.

"But, Captain," said the able seaman, "you can't sail this ship without me!"

"Look here," said the Doctor sternly. "You may be the best seaman in the world, but on *this* ship you are a plain nuisance. I am going to put you ashore at the nearest port!"

"Consider yourself lucky," Polynesia added, "that the Doctor does not have you locked up for stowing away and eating all our salt beef!"

"I don't know what we're going to do now," I heard her whisper to Bumpo. "We've no money to buy any more, and that salt beef was the most important part of the stores."

# POLYNESIA HAS A PLAN

I took the wheel from the Doctor while he made calculations on his map. "Looks like we'll have to run for Capa Blancas after all. I'd sooner swim back to Puddleby than have to listen to that fellow's talk all the way to Brazil."

The Doctor was right. Ben Butcher was a terrible person. According to him, everything we did on the ship was wrong. Ben's criticism made me nervous. "Do you think we're safe without a seaman?" I asked.

"You're always safe with John Dolittle," Polynesia said. "It's true the Doctor does everything wrong, but you always get there, no matter what. And he always has extraordinary good luck. Besides, I have a plan."

"What is it?" Jip asked.

"Is there a key in that door?" she asked, pointing to the dining room door. We looked and found there was.

"Now, Bumpo lays the table for lunch. We all go hide. At twelve o'clock Bumpo rings the dinner bell. Ben will be down expecting more salt beef. Bumpo must hide behind the door outside. As soon as Ben is seated, Bumpo slams the door and locks it. Then we've got him!"

"How stratagenious!" Bumpo chuckled. "I'll lay the table."

"And don't leave any eatables around," Polynesia added.

We all went and hid ourselves where we could watch. Bumpo rang the dinner bell like mad and hid behind the dining room door. Immediately Ben Butcher was heard thumping down the steps. He walked into the dining saloon, sat down at the head of the table in the Doctor's place and tucked a napkin under his chin.

Then, *bang!* Bumpo slammed the door and locked it. "That settles *him* for a while," Polynesia laughed, as she climbed on my shoulder and we went onto the deck.

# THE BEDMAKER OF MONTEVERDE

Ne stayed three days in the Capa Blanca Islands for two reasons. One was the shortage of provisions caused by Ben Butcher's huge appetite. The second was the bullfight.

In these islands, which belonged to Spain, bullfights were held every Sunday. We arrived on a Friday. After getting rid of the seaman, we walked through the town, which was called Monteverde. Streets were narrow, winding and twisting. Houses were so close together that the people could shake hands with their neighbors on the other side of the street.

We did not go to a hotel because we had no money. On the second night, we passed a bedmaker's shop. Several beds the man had made were outside on the street. The Doctor started chatting in Spanish to the bedmaker. As suppertime approached, the man invited

JOSE VILLEGAS:CA

*The Doctor started chatting in Spanish to the bedmaker.*

us to supper. After supper we sat on the pavement and talked far into the night.

When we got up to go back to the ship, the bed-maker wouldn't hear of it. He invited us to sleep in the beds he made on the street. It was hot, so we needed no blankets. And it was great fun to fall asleep outdoors, watching the people walking by. It seemed the Spanish people never went to sleep. Little restaurants and cafes around us were open, and people drank coffee and talked. A guitar softly strummed in the distance, and I fell asleep thinking of my mother and father.

The Seventh Chapter

# THE DOCTOR'S WAGER

The next morning we were awakened by a procession of men in brightly colored clothes, followed by crowds of ladies and cheering children, marching down the street. I asked the Doctor who they were.

"Those men are the bullfighters," he said. "There is to be a bullfight tomorrow."

When I asked what a bullfight was, the Doctor's face reddened with anger. "It is a stupid, cruel, disgusting business," he said. "The Spanish people are most lovable and hospitable. I cannot understand how they enjoy these wretched bullfights."

He explained how a bull was made very angry by teasing. The men would come out waving red cloaks and would then run away. Then they would send poor old horses into the ring for the bull to chase and kill. When the bull was tired, a man came out with a sword and killed him. The Doctor said that every Sunday in every big Spanish town, six bulls and many horses were killed that way.

"Aren't the men ever killed by the bull?" I asked.

"Very seldom," he said. "A bull is not nearly as dangerous as he looks. The bullfighters are clever and quick. A famous bullfighter is more important in Spain than a king. Ridiculous!"

Just then the bedmaker came out to watch the procession. While we were talking, the bedmaker's friend walked up and was introduced as Don Enrique Cárdenas. He spoke in English when he heard where we were from. He seemed very gentlemanly.

He asked if the Doctor planned to go to the bullfight. "Certainly not!" John Dolittle said firmly. "Bullfights are cruel, cowardly shows."

Don Enrique nearly exploded. He said bullfighting was a noble sport.

"Rubbish!" snorted the Doctor. "You never give the poor bull a chance. Only when he is tired and dazed do your matadors dare try to kill him."

It looked as if the Spaniard would strike the Doctor. The bedmaker came between them and took the Doctor aside. He whispered that the Don was an important person. He supplied all the bulls from his own farm for all the bullfights in the Capa Blancas.

The Doctor turned to Don Enrique with a gleam of boyish mischief in his eyes. "You tell me your bullfighters are brave and skillful. Who is the best matador for tomorrow's show?"

"Pepito de Malaga," the Spaniard said. "One of the bravest men in all of Spain."

"I have a proposal. I have never fought a bull. Suppose I went into the ring tomorrow with Pepito and any matadors you choose. If I can do more tricks with a bull than they can, would you promise to do something for me?"

Don Enrique laughed heartily. "You must be mad! You would be killed at once."

"I'll risk it . . . or are you afraid to take my offer?" the Doctor said, smiling.

"Afraid! Sir, if you can beat Pepito de Malaga in the bullring, I'll promise anything I can grant."

"Very good," said the Doctor. "You are a very powerful man. If you wished to stop all bullfighting in these islands after tomorrow you could."

"Yes, I could," Don Enrique said proudly.

"Well, that is what I ask if I win my wager," said the Doctor.

The men shook hands. "I warn you," the Spaniard said, "you are throwing your life away."

He turned and walked into the shop with the bedmaker.

Polynesia flew onto my shoulder. "I have a plan," she whispered into my ear. "Get Bumpo. Come someplace where the Doctor can't hear us."

We pretended to look into a jeweler's window, while the Doctor sat down on the bed to lace his boots.

"This is a great way for us to get some money to buy food," Polynesia said. "The Doctor is bound to win tomorrow. Bumpo, you go to Don Enrique and make a bet that the Doctor will win. He will have to pay you when he loses the bet, which he surely will. Say you will bet him two thousand five hundred pesetas."

We crossed the street and slipped into the bed-maker's shop. The Doctor was still working on his boots.

"Don Enrique, allow me to introduce myself. I am the Crown Prince of Jolliginki. Would you care to have a small bet on tomorrow's bullfight?" Bumpo asked.

Don Enrique bowed. "Why, certainly. But I must warn you that you are bound to lose. How much?"

"A mere truffle," Bumpo said. "Just for fun. Say three thousand pesetas?"

"Agreed," said the Spaniard, bowing. "I will meet you after the bullfight tomorrow."

Polynesia sighed. "I feel as if a huge load has been taken off my mind," she cackled.

# THE GREAT BULLFIGHT

The streets of Monteverde were hung with flags as crowds flocked to the bullring the next day.

The Doctor borrowed a colorful matador's suit from Don Enrique. Bumpo and I worked hard to get the waistcoat to close in front.

Crowds of small boys ran after us as we walked from the harbor with the Doctor. They called him *"Juan Hagapoco, el grueso matador!"*, which is Spanish for "John Dolittle, the fat bullfighter!"

When we arrived, the Doctor said he would like to take a look at the bulls before the fight. In the bull pen, six huge black bulls were running around wildly. In a few hurried words and signs, the Doctor told them what he was going to do. The poor bulls were so happy when they heard there was a chance that bull-fighting would be stopped, they promised to do just what he said.

The Doctor went to the matadors' dressing rooms. Bumpo, Polynesia and I took our seats in the bullring. The ring was crackling with excitement.

At the opening, Don Enrique explained to the crowd the challenge between the Doctor and the matador. He told them what he had promised to do if the Doctor won. The crowd roared with laughter.

Everyone cheered when Pepito entered the ring. A large door across the ring opened, and a bull came charging out.

Pepito waved his red cloak, and the bull rushed toward him. He stepped aside, and the people cheered. The game was repeated for several minutes. Ten minutes later, another small door opened and Doctor Dolittle walked into the ring. The crowd rocked with laughter at the sight of the short, fat matador bulging from his sky-blue velvet suit.

Juan Hagapoco, as they called him, walked to the center of the ring. He bowed to the ladies. He bowed to the bull. He bowed to Pepito and Pepito's assistant as well. Then the bull was let loose.

The Doctor turned, stared at the onrushing bull, and frowned.

The bull's speed slowed, as though he feared the frown. Soon he stopped altogether. The Doctor shook his finger at the bull, who began to tremble. Tucking his tail between his legs, the bull turned and ran away.

A gasp came from the crowd. The Doctor ran after the bull. After ten laps around the ring, the Doctor caught the bull by the tail.

He led him to the center of the ring and made him do circus tricks. He made the bull kneel, and he got on the bull's back and did handsprings and acrobatics on the beast's horns.

Pepito and his assistant grew green with envy as they watched the Doctor.

"This bull is no good anymore," the Doctor said. "Take him away!" He turned toward Don Enrique.

"Does the *caballero* wish for a fresh bull?" the Spaniard asked.

"No. I want five fresh bulls. All in the ring at once," the Doctor said as the crowd hummed with anticipation.

Pepito jumped up and said it was against the rules of bullfighting. The Doctor turned to Pepito and said, "Well, if the *caballero* is afraid—"

"Afraid!" screamed Pepito. "I am afraid of nothing! I have killed nine hundred and fifty-seven bulls!"

"Let's see if you can handle five more," the Doctor shouted. "Let the bulls in!"

As the five bulls bounded into the ring, silence filled the air.

*. . . did handsprings and acrobatics on the beast's horns.*

"Look fierce!" the Doctor called in cattle language. "Go for Pepito, the one in purple, first. But don't kill him, just chase him out of the ring."

The bulls put their heads down and charged straight for Pepito.

The Spaniard tried to look brave. But the sight of the five pairs of horns galloping at him was too much. He turned toward the fence, vaulted over it and disappeared.

"Now the other one," the Doctor whispered. In two seconds the assistant matador was out of sight. Juan Hagapoco, the fat matador, was alone in the ring with five raging bulls.

The rest of the show was really worth seeing. The bulls raced around, bellowing with rage, and shot across the ring, pretending they were ready to toss the Doctor into the sky.

I held my breath, although I knew what had been planned. The bulls all came near to striking the Doctor. But at the last minute, the fat matador jumped out of the way and the brutes thundered past, missing him by a hair.

Then the five bulls encircled him as the crowds screamed with delight. The Doctor broke loose from the animals surrounding him. Catching each by the horn, he gave their heads a sudden twist and threw them into the sand. The bulls acted their parts, panting and growling as if they were exhausted.

With a final bow to the ladies, the Doctor took a cigar from his pocket, lit it and strutted out of the ring.

# WE DEPART IN A HURRY

T he most tremendous noise I ever heard broke
loose as the gate closed behind the Doctor. Some men
were angry, but the ladies called for the Doctor to come
back into the ring.

When he did, the women blew kisses and tossed
flowers, rings, necklaces and brooches at his feet.

The Doctor smiled, bowed and backed out.

"Bumpo," Polynesia ordered. "You go and gather
those trinkets and we'll sell 'em. Then go get your
three thousand pesetas from the Don. Tommy and I
will meet you outside and we'll pawn the stuff at the
jewelry store. Hurry!"

Outside the ring was great excitement. People were
arguing violently. Bumpo met us, his pockets bulging

with jewelry. We slowly slid through the crowd to the matador's dressing room.

"Great work!" Polynesia said to the Doctor. "But I smell danger. Let's get back to the ship quickly. Put your coat over that silly suit. Too many in this crowd are furious because you won. Now they have to stop the bullfighting. We must get away."

"You're right," the Doctor said. "I'll slip down to the ship and wait for you there. Come a different way. Hurry!"

As soon as the Doctor left, Bumpo found Don Enrique. "Honorable sir, you owe me three thousand pesetas," Bumpo said solemnly.

Without a word, the Spaniard paid his debt.

We set out to buy food, hiring a cab along the way. We bought everything in sight at a big grocer's shop. But as we came out of the shop and loaded the cab, we saw crowds of angry men with sticks shouting, "The Englishmen! They stopped the bullfights! Throw them in the sea!"

Bumpo told the driver to take us to the harbor fast. "We won't get to pawn the jewelry," Polynesia said. "But we'll save that for another time. We've got two thousand five hundred pesetas left from the bet."

We reached the harbor. The Doctor had sent Chee-Chee with the rowboat to wait at the landing. As we were moving the supplies from the cab to the boat, the angry mob hit the wharf. Bumpo grabbed a huge beam of wood and swung it around, shrieking dreadfully loud African battle yells. This kept the crowd back while Chee-Chee and I jumped into the boat. Bumpo hurled the beam toward the crowd of Spaniards and leaped in after us. We rowed like mad for the *Curlew*.

The mob howled with rage. We reached the ship's side. The Doctor had the anchor up and everything ready for our getaway. In a moment the *Curlew* swung around into the wind and sped out of the harbor toward Brazil.

"Ha!" sighed Polynesia as we collapsed on the deck and caught our breath. "Not a bad adventure. Not bad at all." And off we went toward our next destination, hoping to find news of Long Arrow on Spider Monkey Island.

# Part IV

# SHELLFISH LANGUAGES AGAIN

$\mathbf{M}$iranda, the purple bird of paradise, had said we'd have good weather. For three weeks the *Curlew* sailed with a steady wind. We did not pass many ships.

One afternoon we saw what looked like dead grass floating around us. The Doctor said it was gulfweed. Many crabs crawled on the weed. The sight of them reminded the Doctor of his dream of learning the language of the shellfish. He fished up several of the crabs and put them in his listening tank. He also caught a strange-looking, chubby little fish called a silver fidgit.

He listened to the crabs with no success. Then he put the fidgit into the tank. I was doing my duties on the deck when I heard him shouting from below to come down.

"Stubbins," he cried, "a most extraordinary thing . . . unbelievable . . . I'm not sure I'm not dreaming. I—I—"

"What is it, Doctor? What's the matter?"

"The fidgit," he whispered, pointing with a trembling finger. "He talks English! And . . . he *whistles tunes—English tunes!*"

"That's impossible!" I cried.

"He speaks only a few words all mixed up with his own language, which I can't make out," said the Doctor. "But they're English words. Listen. Tell me everything you hear."

I went to the glass tank. The Doctor grabbed a notebook and a pencil. I stood on the stand and put my right ear into the water.

At first I heard nothing at all. Then, from within the water, I heard a thin, small voice.

"What is it?" the Doctor asked in a whisper. "What does he say?"

"I can't tell. It's some strange fish language. Wait a minute! Now I get it: 'No smoking' . . . 'My, here's a queer one!' . . . 'Popcorn and picture postcards here' . . . 'This way out' . . . 'Don't spit'—what funny things to say, Doctor!"

"This is most extraordinary!" he kept muttering as his pencil wiggled over the page. "Frightfully thrilling! I wonder where he—"

*"He talks English!"*

"Here's some more English!" I cried. "'The big tank needs cleaning.'"

"'The big tank,'" the Doctor murmured. "Where on earth did he learn—" He leaped out of his chair.

"I have it!" he yelled. "This fish has escaped from an aquarium! Look at the things he has said. There's no doubt about it, Stubbins. It's quite possible—not certain —but possible that through him I may learn the shell-fish language. What a great piece of luck!"

# THE FIDGIT'S STORY

ow that he was started, there was no stopping
the Doctor. He worked through the night. I fell asleep
in my chair around midnight.

Bumpo dozed off at the wheel about two in the
morning. For five hours the *Curlew* drifted unattended as John Dolittle worked on, struggling to
understand the fidgit and make the fidgit understand him.

I awoke to broad daylight. The Doctor stood at the
listening tank, beaming with pride.

"Stubbins," he said, smiling. "I've got it! It's very difficult and different from anything I ever heard. It isn't
shellfish, but a giant leap toward it.

"I want you to write down everything I say," he continued. "The fidgit is going to tell me the story of his life, and I will translate it to English. Ready?"

The Doctor put his ear under the water and relayed the story of the fidgit's thirteen months in an aquarium.

The fidgit was born near the coast of Chile in the Pacific, one of 2,510 fidgits in his family. He and his sister, Clippa, escaped when the family was broken up by a herd of whales. They fled up the coast of South America and headed up the west coast of the United States. While swimming in a harbor, they were caught in a net by some fishermen and taken to a house on the edge of the harbor filled with large boxes of water containing different kinds of fish.

They hated living inside the water boxes, where there was nothing to do but watch the people who came to stare at them.

The fidgits wondered if the people could talk, and they watched their lips move. Over time, they learned several of the phrases the people always used, like "Oh, look, here's a queer one!", although they never understood what it meant.

The keepers pointed to signs that read DON'T SPIT or NO SMOKING, and after a while the fidgits learned to read the signs.

They lived in the building, which was called an aquarium, for a whole year. One day the fidgit suggested to his sister that they pretend to be sick or dead. Maybe then they would be thrown back into the sea.

The next morning the keepers found both fidgits floating dead on the water. It was hard for the fidgits to keep still and not breathe. A man carried them from the building and tried to dump them in a garbage can but was stopped by a policeman. He looked around for a place to throw them and, seeing none, tossed them back into the harbor. They had escaped! Shrieking with delight, they sped for the open sea and home.

The Doctor told the fidgit he would release him as soon as he answered some questions about shellfish for him. The fidgit agreed.

He told the Doctor that he could not speak shellfish language. He did say that shellfish had small, thin voices. He suggested that the best way for the Doctor to get to the bottom of the sea to talk to the shellfish was to find the great glass sea snail. This was an enormous salt-water snail whose shell was made of transparent mother-of-pearl. The fidget said the great glass sea snail's shell was big enough to carry a wagon and two horses!

"That is just the creature I have been looking for!" the Doctor exclaimed. "He could take us inside his shell to explore the deepest depths. Do you think you could get him for me?"

The fidgit said he would if he could, but he did not go into the Deep Hole under the sea where the great glass sea snail spent most of his time.

"That's a terrible disappointment," the Doctor sighed. "What wonderful things he could tell me!"

Then the fidgit told the Doctor he was anxious to get back into seawater. Reluctantly the Doctor carried the listening tank to the porthole, thanked the fidgit and emptied the tank into the sea.

I was exhausted from writing down the conversation, but the Doctor was even more tired. Within moments he dropped into a chair, closed his eyes and began to snore.

Polynesia scratched angrily at the door. I tiptoed outside to find her enraged that the ship had been cruising unattended all night.

I put the notebook carefully in a drawer and hurried to the deck to take the wheel.

**The Third Chapter**

# BAD WEATHER

I took the wheel and immediately noticed we weren't going as fast as we had been. Our wind had almost entirely disappeared.

At first we didn't worry, figuring the wind would start up again soon. But one whole day went by, then two, then a week, then ten days. There was no wind. The Doctor was becoming uneasy.

One afternoon I found him mumbling to himself about the misty appearance of the sky. "The purple bird of paradise will understand if we're late," I said. "And we've plenty to eat on board. It will be all right."

"I suppose so," he said thoughtfully. "I hate to keep Miranda waiting, though. She goes to the Peruvian mountains for her health this time of year." A small breeze blew from the northeast.

Suddenly the wind changed quickly, swinging east, then northeast, then north. Fitful gusts kept me busy at the wheel, swinging the ship this way and that to keep it upright.

From the lookout above, Polynesia screeched down, "Bad weather's coming! That black line over in the east is storm clouds!"

She flew down to the deck. "I think you should take the wheel from Tommy," she said to the Doctor. "It'll need a strong arm if it's a real storm. I'll wake Bumpo and Chee-Chee."

The sky suddenly darkened, and the black line to the east came closer and closer. A low, rumbling noise moaned over the sea. The beautiful blue water turned a murky gray.

I was frightened. Until this moment I had seen only a friendly sea. But I had not known, or even guessed at, the sea's terrible anger.

The storm struck. The *Curlew* leaned right over, flat on its side as though slapped by an invisible hand. The wind howled, and the water hit hard. I don't remember exactly what happened, but the *Curlew* was shipwrecked.

The sails flew out of our hands as we tried to roll them. Huge waves swelled like nightmare monsters, crashing on the ship and into the sea.

I clambered along the deck toward the Doctor, clinging with hands and legs to the railing so I wouldn't be blown overboard. Suddenly a huge wave hit, and I lost hold. My throat filled with water, and I was swept the length of the deck. My head hit a door with a thud. And then I fainted.

## The Fourth Chapter

# WRECKED!

The sky was blue and the sea was calm when I awoke. My head throbbed. I thought I must have fallen asleep on the deck of the ship. I tried to get up.

I couldn't move. My arms were tied to something behind me with a piece of rope. I twisted around and saw a piece of broken mast.

Then I realized I wasn't sitting on the ship at all, only on a piece of it. I was scared. I searched the sea all around me. I was alone in the ocean!

Slowly I remembered what had happened. But where were the Doctor and the others?

I worked my hand into my pocket and got my penknife to cut the rope. It reminded me of one of Joe's shipwreck stories about a captain who tied up his

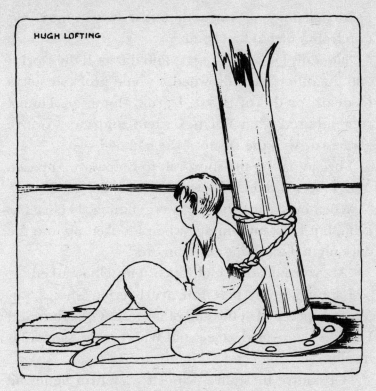

*I was alone in the ocean!*

son so he wouldn't be washed away in a gale. The Doctor must have done the same to me.

But where was he?

He and the others couldn't be drowned! I stood up shakily and stared around at the sea. Nothing but water and sky. Suddenly I spotted a bird skimming low over the water. It was a stormy petrel. I tried to talk to it, but I didn't know enough seabird language.

It circled my raft twice, then flew away in the direction from which it had come.

Suddenly I was very hungry and thirsty. If the Doctor and the others were drowned, I would probably starve to death or die of thirst. I grew gloomier. Then I remembered what Polynesia had told me. "You're always safe with the Doctor," she had said.

I began pacing the short raft to keep warm. I paced until I was so tired I lay down and fell asleep on the raft.

When I woke up, the stars were shining. The sea was calm, but I lost my courage when I looked up into the dark night. I was hungrier than ever!

"Are you awake?" a high voice at my elbow asked.

I sprang to my feet and nearly cried when I saw Miranda perched at the end of my raft. "Oh, Miranda!" I cried. "I'm so glad to see you! Where is the Doctor? Is he alive?"

"Of course he's alive—and it's my firm belief he always will be. He's about forty miles westward."

"Thank heavens! And Bumpo and the animals . . . are they all right?"

"Yes. They're with him. The ship broke in half during the storm. The Doctor tied you down when he found you. What a storm! I've been watching for your ship for three weeks, but I had to take refuge in a cave last night, it was so bad. As soon as I found the Doctor, he sent me off with some porpoises to find you. The petrel spotted you and told us where you were."

"But how can I get to the Doctor, Miranda?"

"You're going now. Look behind you."

I turned around and saw, at the back of the raft, four porpoises just below the surface, pushing the raft with their noses!

Suddenly I heard Bumpo's enormous voice singing African tunes. I peered toward the sound and made out a dim mass of tattered wreckage, all that was left of the *Curlew*.

# LAND!

I clambered onto the other half of the ship to great greetings. Bumpo gave me a wonderful drink of fresh water from a barrel. Chee-Chee and Polynesia fed me biscuits.

But the sight of the Doctor's smiling face cheered me more than anything. Thanking Miranda for getting me so quickly, he asked her to lead us to Spider Monkey Island. He told the porpoises to follow the bird of paradise, pushing the half of our ship we all sat on.

We traveled southward for three days. The farther we went, the colder it got. The Doctor guessed that Spider Monkey Island had been disturbed by the great wind and had drifted farther south than it had ever been before.

146

Miranda came back on the third night, nearly frozen. She said the island would be quite close to us in the morning. The night mist prevented our seeing it. She promised the Doctor she would visit him in Puddleby in August as usual, but said she had to hurry to a warmer climate.

The Doctor thanked her endlessly for all she had done. She wished us good luck and disappeared into the night.

We awakened long before daylight. Polynesia was the first to spot palm trees and mountaintops on what turned out to be a long island with high, rocky mountains in the middle.

The porpoises gave us a final push, and we bumped gently into a low beach. We couldn't wait to get our legs on land for the first time in six weeks—even if it was floating land!

What a thrilling feeling it was for me to know I was standing on the very place my pencil had touched in the atlas just a few weeks earlier!

The porpoises asked the Doctor if he needed them any longer. He thanked them and said no. Then we got ready to explore the island.

Suddenly we saw a band of Indians watching us from behind the trees. The Doctor went to talk to them, but he could not make them understand that we had come on a friendly visit. At last he made them understand that we just wanted to look around and would go away after a while.

Just then another Indian arrived with a message. They shook their spears as they turned and left.

"They're going off to their village," Polynesia whispered. "There is probably another village on the other side of the mountains. I think we should get off this beach and onto higher land. They may grow friendlier when they see we mean no harm. They probably never saw people like us before."

We headed toward the mountains in the center of the island.

# THE JABIZRI

The woods at the foot of the hills were thick and tangly. Polynesia and Chee-Chee were good guides. They set out looking for food for us. Soon they found many fruits and nuts that made great eating. We also discovered a clean stream of water to drink.

We followed the stream up and came to a place where the woods were thinner, the ground rocky and steep. We saw wonderful views all over the island.

Suddenly the Doctor said, "Shhh! A jabizri! Don't you hear it?"

We listened and heard an extraordinary musical hum—like a bee. It rose and fell, like someone singing.

"No other insect but the jabizri beetle hums like that," the Doctor said. "I wonder where he is. Quite near, by the sound—if only I had my butterfly net! Confound that storm! I may miss the chance of a lifetime to get the rarest beetle in the world. Oh, look! There he goes!"

A huge beetle, at least three inches long, suddenly flew by our noses. The Doctor got so excited, he took off his hat to use as a net, swooped at the beetle and caught it! He knelt down with the jabizri safely under his hat. From his pocket he took out a glass-topped box and guided the beetle into it.

It was a beautiful insect, pale blue underneath, with a glossy black back and huge red spots.

"Ho, look! This jabizri's got something on his leg!" the Doctor exclaimed.

He carefully took the beetle by its back and pointed to something rolled around the middle section of its right foreleg that resembled a thin, dried leaf. It was neatly tied with a strong spiderweb.

His fingers deftly untied the cobweb cord and unrolled the leaf without tearing it or hurting the beetle. He put the jabizri back in the box, spread out the leaf and examined it.

Inside, the tiny leaf was covered with signs and pictures so small you needed a magnifying glass to see them. Most were figures of men and mountains in a strange brown ink.

Everyone stared at the leaf. "This is written in blood," Doctor Dolittle said at last. "That's the color it turns when dry. I wish I talked beetle language so I could find out where it was from! These drawings are a message. But why give it to the jabizri, the rarest beetle in the world?" he muttered. "There are men walking up a mountain, into a hole, pointing to their mouths, prison bars, maybe. This looks like men praying and lying down. And this, a peculiar-shaped mountain."

Suddenly a smile of understanding spread across the Doctor's face. *"Long Arrow!"* he cried. "Why, of course! Only a naturalist would think of giving this letter to the rarest of all beetles, one other naturalists would try to catch! This must be the only kind of writing he knows."

"But what does it say?" I asked.

"First," the Doctor said, "it shows men going up a mountain. That's Long Arrow and his party. Then going into a mountain, looking for plants or mosses in a cave. Then a mountain falling down, trapping them. And *this* was the only way to get a message out—with a beetle who could burrow out into the open air."

He sprang to his feet. "This is their cry for help. Come! Up the mountain, all of you. Bumpo, bring the water and nuts. Let's hope we're not too late!"

"Where are you going to look?" I asked.

"Look at the last picture, the oddly shaped mountain—like a hawk's head. We must get on a high peak and find a mountain shaped like that. To delay could mean Long Arrow's death!"

# HAWK'S HEAD MOUNTAIN

fterward, we agreed we had never worked so hard in our lives. We scrambled to the top of the high peak. Instantly we saw the mountain drawn in the letter. It was the second-highest mountain on the island.

With one look at the sun for directions, the Doctor dashed down, not stopping to catch his breath. Bumpo and I followed as fast as we could. The animals were in front of the Doctor, enjoying the hunt. We reached the foot of the mountain.

"Now we will separate and search for caves," the Doctor said. "We will meet in this spot in an hour. Shout if you find anything."

Each was anxious to be the one to make the discovery. The mountain was searched thoroughly but no one found a fallen-in cave.

One by one, tired and disappointed, we straggled back to the meeting place. The Doctor was gloomy.

"Jip," he said, "couldn't you *smell* any men anywhere?"

"I sniffed every crack in the mountain," Jip said. "But the air here is saturated with the smell of spider monkeys. It drowns every other scent. And it's too cold and dry for good smelling."

"And getting colder all the time," the Doctor agreed. "I'm afraid this island is drifting even farther southward. Chee-Chee, did you have any luck?"

"Nothing, Doctor. I climbed every peak and searched every hollow."

"Polynesia, did you see anything?"

"No," she said. "But I have a plan. Do you still have that beetle, the biz-biz, or whatever?" she asked.

"Yes, right here." The Doctor pulled out the glass-topped box.

"All right," she said. "Now, if what you suppose is true, Long Arrow found that beetle *inside* the cave, since he was hunting plants, not beetles, right?"

The Doctor nodded.

"Then it's fair to suppose that the beetle's home is in the cave or hole where the Indians are trapped."

"Quite, quite."

"So, let the beetle go. Sooner or later he'll go back to Long Arrow's cave. We'll follow him. Then we'll know which part of the mountain we need."

"But he may fly if I let him out," the Doctor said.

"*Let* him fly! A parrot can wing it as fast as a biz-biz any day!"

"Polynesia, you have a truly great brain," said the Doctor.

Polynesia added, "Why not put a message to Long Arrow on the beetle's leg, saying we're trying to get to him?"

"Splendid!" the Doctor said, instantly putting tiny pictures on a dry leaf he pulled from a nearby bush.

At last Mr. Jabizri was ready to go. He crawled off the Doctor's finger, stretched his legs and headed leisurely to the west.

We expected him to walk *up* the mountain. Instead, he walked *around* it. As hours dragged by, we wished he would fly so Polynesia could chase after it.

After leading us all around the mountain, he stopped at the exact spot where we had started from and didn't move.

"His home must be near here," Polynesia said. "That's why he's come back."

"Then why did he go all around the mountain first?" I asked.

"Look! Look!" the Doctor called out. The jabizri was climbing *up* the mountain at a much faster pace.

When he was no more than ten feet above our heads, he sudddenly disappeared into the face of the rock.

"There must be a hole up there," Polynesia said, fluttering up the rock and clinging to the face of it with her claws. "Right here, about two fingers wide."

The Doctor picked up a huge stone and banged it with all his might against the face of the rock. It made a hollow, booming sound.

Suddenly my spine tingled, as three answering knocks came from within: *Boom!* . . . *Boom!* . . . *Boom!*

"Thank heaven!" the Doctor said, breaking the hushed silence. "Some of them are alive!"

*He banged it with all his might against the face of the rock.*

# Part V

# A GREAT MOMENT

We all scrambled around looking for an opening or crevice to work on. Scratching at the foot of the slab, Jip made the discovery that led to success.

"Doctor!" he cried. "The slab is only resting on a bed of soft earth. It's easy digging. If we scratch the earth from under, the slab might drop and the Indians can climb over the top."

"You're right," the Doctor said, examining the earth bed. "Let's get at it!"

The whole crew squatted, scratching and burrowing at the foot of the mountain. After about an hour, the Doctor said, "Be ready to jump from under if the slab falls."

Suddenly there was a grating, grinding sound.

*159*

"Look out!" yelled the Doctor. "Scatter! Here she comes!"

The big rock slid down about a foot. There were no signs of a cave within, but we heard human voices. Then suddenly, with a roaring crash that shook the whole mountain range, the slab struck the earth and cracked in half.

We saw the black mouth of a twenty-foot-high tunnel. In the center stood a handsome, seven-foot-tall man, slim and muscular, wearing a beaded cloth about his middle and an eagle's feather in his hair. He held one hand up to shield his face from the blinding sun.

"It is he," he Doctor whispered. "I know by his great height and the scar on his chin."

He stepped forward across the fallen stone, his hand outstretched to Long Arrow. The Indian uncovered his eyes. Slowly he raised his right arm and took the Doctor's hand in his. It was a great moment.

The Doctor tried to speak, but Long Arrow knew no English and the Doctor knew no Indian. He tried several animal languages, but Long Arrow did not know them. Finally he came to the language of the eagles.

"Great Long Arrow," he said in the fierce screams and short grunts that the big birds use, "never have I been so glad in all my life as I am today to find you still alive."

In a flash, Long Arrow's face lit with a smile of understanding. In the eagle tongue he replied, "Mighty

*It was a great moment.*

friend, I owe my life to you. For the rest of my days I am your servant."

The Doctor signaled to Bumpo, who came forward with nuts and water. Long Arrow didn't eat any. He nodded his thanks to Bumpo and carried the food and water into the cave. We followed.

Inside were nine other Indians, men, women and boys, lying on the rock floor, thin and exhausted. Quickly the Doctor went around, listening to their hearts. All were alive, but one woman was so weak, she could not stand up. The Doctor sent Chee-Chee and Polynesia into the jungle for more fruit and water.

Suddenly we heard a sound outside the cave. Clustered at the entrance was the band of Indians we had met on the beach that morning.

They peered into the dark cave cautiously. As soon as they saw Long Arrow and the others, they came rushing in, laughing with joy. Long Arrow explained to Doctor Dolittle that the Indians with him were two families who had come into the mountains to help gather medicinal plants.

While they were searching for a special plant that only grows inside damp caves, the great rock slab had slid down and trapped them.

For two weeks they lived on the medicinal moss and any fresh water that dripped inside the cave. The Indians on the island mourned them all as dead.

Long Arrow told the other Indians that the Doctor and his friends had freed their relatives. They gathered around John Dolittle, talking and beating their breasts in apology for their attitude that morning.

Since then, travelers to Spider Monkey Island tell me that the stone slab is a regular sight the Indian guides show. Their story of how it got there is that, when the Doctor found that his friend Long Arrow was trapped inside the cave, he was so angry he ripped the mountain in half with his bare hands to get him out!

**The Second Chapter**

# THE MEN OF THE MOVING LAND

The Indians were very nice to us. We were invited to their village for a feast in honor of the rescue of the lost families and Long Arrow.

On the way down the mountain, the Indians told Long Arrow something that appeared to be sad news. The Doctor asked what was wrong. Long Arrow said the chief of the tribe had died that morning.

"What did he die of?" the Doctor asked.

"The cold," Long Arrow sighed.

We were all shivering as the sun set. "This is quite serious," the Doctor said to me. "If nothing can be done, the Indians might have to take to their canoes and abandon the island. Otherwise, they might freeze to death from the Antarctic ice."

We came to the top of the hills. Down on the far side of the island was the village, a large cluster of grass huts and brightly colored totem poles near the edge of the sea.

"How artistic!" the Doctor said. "What is the name of the village?"

"Popsipetel," said Long Arrow. "Which is also the name of the tribe. In our language it means 'men of the moving land.' There are two tribes on the island: the Popsipetels at this end and the Bag-jagderags at the other."

"Which one is larger?"

"By far the Bag-jagderags," said Long Arrow as a frown darkened his handsome face. "But I would take one Popsipetel over one hundred Bag-jagderags."

When told how the strange visitor had made the rescue, the entire village gathered around the Doctor, shaking his hands and patting his back. They lifted him on their strong shoulders and carried him down the hill into the center of the village.

The welcome there was even more wonderful. In spite of the cold air of the coming night, the villagers came out by the hundreds.

We were presented with a brand-new grass house, clean and sweet-smelling. Six strong Indian boys were assigned to be our servants.

Inside our new home we found a feast of fish and fruit. Long Arrow invited us to sit down and eat. We were all hungry but were surprised and disappointed when we found out the fish was raw.

The Doctor apologized and explained to Long Arrow that we would prefer our fish cooked. Imagine our surprise when we learned that Long Arrow did not know what the word *cooked* meant!

Polynesia pulled on the Doctor's sleeve.

"You know what's wrong here," she observed. "These people don't know how to make a fire. *They have no fire!*"

# FIRE

The Doctor asked Long Arrow if he knew what fire was. Long Arrow said he had seen it coming from the tops of volcanoes. He and the other Popsipetels did not know how it was made.

"No wonder the old chief died of cold!" muttered Bumpo.

There was a crying sound at the door, and a weeping Indian mother carrying a baby said something to Long Arrow. He told the Doctor the baby was sick and she wanted him to try and cure it.

"Just like Puddleby," Polynesia groaned, "right in the middle of dinner. Well, at least here the food's raw so it can't get cold."

The Doctor examined the baby and said it was thoroughly chilled. "Fire—that's what the baby and the whole village needs. This child will get pneumonia if it isn't kept warm."

"But how do we make fire?" asked Long Arrow.

We hunted through our pockets to see if any matches had survived the shipwreck. None had.

"There are ways to make fire without matches," the Doctor said. "One is with a strong glass and the rays of the sun. But since the sun has set that is no good. Another is by grinding a hard stick into a soft log. Since the daylight is gone, we'll have to wait until morning to get the different wood, as well as an old squirrel's nest for fuel," the Doctor said.

"But all fireless people can see in the dark!" Long Arrow said. "I will send a messenger and we shall have a squirrel's nest within the hour."

He gave an order to two of the servants, who ran out of the hut. In a very short time, a squirrel's nest, as well as both hard and soft woods, were brought to our door.

The moon had not yet risen. It was pitch black within the house. I could feel and hear, though, that the Indians moved comfortably about as though it were daylight.

Using a bow, the Doctor loosened the string, put the hard stick into a loop, and started grinding it into the soft wood of the log. Soon the smell of the smoking log filled the room. He kept feeding the part that was smoking with the inside lining of the squirrel's nest. He asked me to blow on it. He drilled the stick faster and faster. More smoke filled the room. Suddenly the darkness turned to light when the squirrel's nest burst into flame.

The Indians murmured with astonishment. They fell on their knees. They wanted to touch it with their bare hands and play with it. We had to teach them how to use it.

They were awed when we laid our fish across it on sticks and cooked it. They sniffed the air and smiled. For the first time in history, the smell of fried fish passed through the village of Popsipetel.

We asked them to bring piles and stacks of dry wood to the center of the main street, and we made an enormous bonfire. The whole tribe gathered around, smiling in wonder when they felt the warmth.

When we had shown them how to handle the fire, the Doctor said it could be taken into their houses if holes were made in the roofs to let out the smoke. And before we went to sleep, fires were going in every hut in the village.

# WHAT MAKES AN ISLAND FLOAT?

After that, the Doctor was so popular that crowds of admirers followed him wherever he went. After his fire making, they expected him always to do magic, and they didn't want to miss a thing.

We escaped from the crowd that first morning and set out with Long Arrow to explore the island.

We found that plants and trees were suffering from the cold. Animal life was in even worse shape. Shivering birds gathered together for flight to warmer lands. Many lay dead on the ground. Icebergs floated to the southeast, a sign that the island was not far from the Antarctic.

Looking out to sea, we saw the porpoises. The Doctor hailed them, and they came in to shore. The Doctor explained that the island was floating southward when it belonged in a tropical zone. "If it doesn't get warmer, everything will perish," he said.

"Well," said the porpoises, "the whales could push it to a warmer climate—if you got enough of them."

"What a splendid idea! Do you think you could get me some?"

"Certainly," said the porpoises, "we passed a herd coming here."

"Thank you," said the Doctor. "You are always so kind." Then he asked if they knew how the island came to be a floating one.

They said it used to be a mountainous corner of South America. Thousands of years ago, it had broken off from the mainland and got filled with air inside when it fell into the ocean. A huge air chamber, which ran right through the mountains, was what kept it floating.

"What a pecurious phenometer!" Bumpo said.

"Indeed," agreed the Doctor, taking out his notebook and jotting it down.

The porpoises took off to find the whales and soon returned with at least two hundred of them. They were enormous creatures!

"Here they are," said the porpoises.

"Good!" said the Doctor. "Just explain to them how serious this is for all the living creatures of this land. Ask them to go to the far end of the island, put their noses against it and push it back near the southern coast of Brazil."

Soon the whales were thrashing through the sea to the south end of the island. We lay down on the beach and waited.

After about an hour, the Doctor threw a stick into the water. For a while it floated without moving. Soon we saw it begin to move gently down the coast.

"Thank goodness!" the Doctor said with a smile. "The island is going north at last." Faster and faster we went, leaving the stick behind. Soon the icebergs grew dim along the skyline.

The Doctor threw more sticks in and looked at his watch.

"Good work. Fourteen and a half knots an hour. A nice speed. We should be back near Brazil in about five days," he said. "I feel warmer already. Let's go and get something to eat!"

**The Fifth Chapter**

# WAR!

On our way back to the village, an Indian runner came racing up with a message.

Long Arrow listened gravely. He turned to the Doctor and in the eagle tongue said, "Great Doctor, our neighbors to the south, the thievish Bag-jagderags, are right now advancing to attack us. They want to steal our stores of ripe corn."

"Evil news, to be sure," said the Doctor. "But maybe they are desperate for food because the frost killed their harvest."

"Make no excuses for the Bag-jagderags," Long Arrow said. "They are lazy. They would not dare to make war upon us except that they are a bigger tribe."

The village was in a great state of excitement. Men were readying their bows, spears and battle-axes. Women were erecting a fence of high bamboo poles around the village. Scouts and messengers came and went with news of the enemy.

The Doctor said he would go to the enemy to try to make peace. War, he said, was a stupid, wasteful business. But the Indians said it was hopeless. The last messenger sent to try to make peace had been killed with an ax.

Suddenly the lookout howled a cry of alarm. "They're coming . . . swarming down the mountains in thousands!"

"I don't believe in war," the Doctor said. "But if the village is attacked, we must defend it."

He picked up a club. "This seems like a pretty good tool," he said as he walked to the fence and took his place beside the other waiting fighters.

Everyone got some kind of weapon to help the Popsipetels. I got a bow and arrows. Jip was relying on his strong teeth. Chee-Chee took a big bag of rocks into a tree to throw at the enemies' heads. Bumpo marched after the Doctor armed with a young tree in one hand and a doorpost in the other.

We gasped when we saw the size of the enemy. "I'm going to get some help!" Polynesia cried.

"She's gone to get the black parrots," Jip said. "Let's hope she finds them in time!"

The village was completely surrounded within fifteen minutes. Things happened so quickly that all I remember is, had it not been for the Terrible Three, as they came to be called, the war would have quickly been lost.

Long Arrow, Bumpo and the Doctor took their place in Popsipetel history that day. The enemy easily knocked down the bamboo fence. But then the Doctor, Long Arrow and Bumpo began their attack. In spite of the odds, the enemy was thrown out. The strength and weight of the three men from different lands, standing close together and swinging their enormous war clubs, was a sight of wonder. Many weeks later while passing a campfire, I heard a song that has since become a traditional folk song of the Popsipetels.

### The Song of the Terrible Three

*Oh, hear ye the song of the Terrible Three*
*And the fight that they fought by the edge of the sea.*
*Down from the mountains, the rocks and the crags,*
*Swarming like wasps, came the Bag-jagderags.*
*Surrounding our village, our walls they broke down.*
*Oh, sad was the plight of our men and our town!*
*But Heaven determined our land to set free*
*And sent us the help of the Terrible Three.*
*Shoulder to shoulder, they hammered and hit.*

*"The Terrible Three"*

*From an Indian rock engraving found on*
*Hawk's Head Mountain, Spider Monkey Island*

*Like demons of fury they kicked and they bit.*
*Like a wall of destruction they stood in a row,*
*Flattening enemies, six at a blow.*
*And long shall we sing of the Terrible Three*
*And the fight that they fought by the edge of the sea.*

# GENERAL POLYNESIA

But even the mighty Three could not last forever against the enemy. The Bag-jagderags broke through the fence, and in the battle Long Arrow was knocked down with a spear in his chest.

Bumpo and the Doctor fought on for another half hour side by side. The quiet, kindly little Doctor was dealing out whacks heard a mile away.

Bumpo was a demon come to life. No one dared come within yards of him. But a small stone struck him in the center of his forehead, and down went the second of the Three.

John Dolittle fought on alone. Suddenly another length of fence crashed down and the enemy poured in like a flood. "Run for your lives!" the Popsipetels cried. "The war is lost!"

I thought the Doctor and I would be trampled to death. But then we heard the most terrifying noise: the sound of millions of parrots screeching together angrily. Polynesia had brought the black parrot army in the nick of time.

The black parrots were coal black except for a scarlet beak and a streak of red in their wings and tails. On command from Polynesia, they set upon the enemy. Four parrots attacked each Bag-jagderag, clipping snips out of their ears. It won the war for the Popsipetels.

Howling pitifully, the Bag-jagderags tried to flee. When the birds were done with them, the Bag-jagderags' ears looked like postage stamps. It did no permanent harm, and later it became the tribal mark of the Bag-jagderags. Scalloped ears were proof that a man had fought in the Great War. And that is how the tribe came to be known as the Ragged-Eared Bag-jagderags.

As soon as the enemy was gone, the Doctor attended to the wounded. There were few serious injuries. Long Arrow was the worst off. But after the Doctor had washed his wound and got him to bed, he said he felt much better. Bumpo was badly stunned but otherwise unhurt.

The Doctor picked up his high hat which had been knocked off in the fight, dusted it carefully, and put it on. The he called to Polynesia and told her to have the black parrots guard the enemy all night. "Tomorrow we will arrange terms of peace, and we will do it in the City of Bag-jagderag!" he said.

The admiring Popsipetels cheered. The war was over.

# THE PEACE OF THE PARROTS

The next day we set out in canoes for the far end of the island. It took twenty-five hours to reach the City of Bag-jagderag!

The Doctor's visit was short. Long Arrow remained at the village, still too weak to travel. The Doctor brought a young Indian boy whom he was teaching to speak English. Between the two of them, he was sure he would get his point across to the Bag-jagderags.

When the Doctor went to shore, the Indians were in a humble mood. The Doctor, Bumpo, the young Indian and I went straight to the palace of the chief.

Important tribesmen stood at the foot of the palace steps, hands outstretched in friendship to the angry Doctor, who marched right past them. He stood at the top of the steps of the palace and gave a long speech to the Indians. He called them cowards, thieves and bullies and said he had not decided whether to have the black parrots drive them all into the sea to rid the land of them.

A cry for mercy rose from the crowd at this. They all fell to their knees and said they would do whatever he asked.

The Doctor called for one of their scribes who did picture-writing. On the stone walls of the palace, he made the scribe write what has become known as *The Peace of the Parrots.* It was very long. The main point was that there was to be no more fighting and that both tribes promised to help one another in case of corn famine or other distress.

The Bag-jagderags were shocked. They had expected from the Doctor's angry face that he would order many people killed and the rest made into slaves. His orders changed their fear to admiration.

They asked him to stay with them and promised him great riches.

He held up his hand for silence. "No man would wish to be your guest until you proved by your deeds that you are honest," he said. "Be true to the terms of the Peace and from yourselves shall come good government and prosperity. Farewell."

He turned, and we followed him back to the canoes.

# THE HANGING STONE

The Doctor made a great impression on the Bag-jagderags, and their change of heart was sincere. In fact, his speech from the palace steps probably had more impact than anything else he did on Spider Monkey Island.

We went ashore about halfway back to Popsipetel and explored the central part of the island for a few days. The Indian paddlers took us up in the mountains to a region called Whispering Rocks, overhanging the sea.

It was like a great basin in the mountains. In the center rose a table of rock with an ivory chair upon it. The mountains rose around it like theater seats, except at one narrow end, which opened to a view of the sea.

*The Whispering Rocks*

The Doctor asked why it was called Whispering
Rocks. The guides said that no matter where you stood,
if you just whispered, your words echoed throughout
the whole theater. They took us up into the great bowl
to try it, explaining that this was where the king was

crowned when the Popsipetels were one people and owned all of Spider Monkey Island.

They pointed out an enormous hanging stone perched on the edge of a volcano's crater. There was a legend that when the greatest of all Popsipetel kings would be crowned, the Hanging Stone would tumble to the center of the earth.

The Doctor wanted a closer look. We walked to the stone, which was as big as a cathedral. Underneath was a black hole that appeared endless. "Stubbins," the Doctor said, "remember when the porpoises told us about the air chamber in the center of the island?"

I nodded. The Doctor said that this stone was heavy enough that if it did fall, the air would escape and the island would sink.

"Wouldn't everyone be drowned?" I asked.

"No. It depends on the depth of the sea. It could go down a hundred feet, but there would still be much land left above the water," he said.

We climbed back into our canoes and headed to the village. We were surprised to find that the whole village had been up all night. The elders of the tribe were voting on a new chief. The name would be announced at midday.

The Doctor went to check on Long Arrow, who was making good progress. We went to our house, ate some breakfast and all lay down for a rest. Moments after our weary heads touched the pillows, we were all asleep.

# THE ELECTION

**M**usic awakened us. The bright noonday sunlight streamed in our door. A band was playing outside.

We got up and looked out. Our house was surrounded by everyone in Popsipetel. They were dressed up in bright beads, gaudy feathers and colorful blankets. The people sang or played painted wooden whistles or drums made from skins.

"The election results were announced," Polynesia said.

"And who is the new chief?" the Doctor asked.

"You are," Polynesia said quietly.

"*I!*" gasped the Doctor. "Well, of all things!"

"You're the one! And they've changed your name, too. *Dolittle* wasn't a proper name for a man who did so much. So now you are Jong Thinkalot. How do you like it?"

"But I don't *want* to be a chief," he said irritably.

"You'll have a tough time getting out of it now," she said. "You've been elected the King of the whole of Spider Monkey Island. The Bag-jagderags insisted they and their lands be united with the Popsipetels' so you could be King to both."

"Bother it, I don't *want* to be King!" groaned the Doctor.

"I should think, Doctor, you'd feel rather proud," I said. "I wish *I* had a chance to be a King."

"Oh, it sounds grand," he said. "But you can't take up responsibilities and then just drop them again when you feel like it. I have my own work to do. If I'm made King of the Popsipetels, that's the end of me as a naturalist. I'd be too busy for anything."

"Look," said Polynesia, "here come the headmen to announce your election. Hurry up and get your boots laced."

The crowd at our door suddenly parted, making a long lane down which a handsome old Indian with a wrinkled face came, carrying an incredibly beautiful wooden crown. Behind him were eight strong Indians bearing a chair with long handles underneath to carry it.

Kneeling down on one knee, his head bent almost to the ground, the old man addressed the Doctor.

"O Mighty One," he said. "Great are your deeds, kind is your heart, and your wisdom is deeper than the sea. Our people need you. Our old enemies, the Bag-jagderags, have become our brothers and friends because of you. I bring to you the Sacred Crown of Popsipetel, which since ancient days has rested on no kingly brow. We are bidden by the united voices of the peoples to carry you to Whispering Rocks. There you may be crowned King of all the Moving Land."

The Indians never even considered that John Dolittle might say no.

"My friends," he said. "I am not worthy of this great honor. Among your own brave men you must find many better fitted to lead you. I thank you for this compliment. But do not think of me for such high duties, which I could not possibly fulfill."

The old man repeated the Doctor's words to the crowd of people behind him. They shook their heads and wouldn't move an inch. The old man turned back to the Doctor.

"You are the chosen one," he said. "They will have none other."

Suddenly a flash of hope crossed the Doctor's perplexed face.

"I'll go and see Long Arrow," he whispered. "Perhaps he will know some way to get me out of this!"

Asking to be excused, he left and hurried off to Long Arrow's house. I followed him.

We found our big friend lying on a grass bed outside his home so he could witness the event.

"Long Arrow," said the Doctor, speaking quickly in the eagle tongue. "I come to you for help. These men would make me King. All the great work I hoped to do as a naturalist would have to go undone. Speak with them and persuade their kind hearts that this is unwise."

Long Arrow raised himself on his elbow.

"O Kindly One," he said. "I can do nothing. These people have their hearts set on you as their King. If I interfered, they would drive me from the land and crown you anyway. You must be a King, if only for a while. Maybe later we will get a plan to relieve you of the burden of the crown. But for now you must be King."

Sadly the Doctor turned away. And there behind him stood the old Indian holding the crown in his wrinkled hands, the royal litter waiting at his elbow. With reverence, the bearers motioned toward the chair, inviting the Doctor to get in.

For a moment I thought the Doctor would run away. But the crowd was thick. A band of whistles and drums suddenly started a processional march.

Almost in tears, John Dolittle stepped slowly onto the litter and sat down, muttering, "I don't *want* to be King!"

Long Arrow called farewell. "May good fortune ever stand within the shadow of your throne," he said.

The procession formed to leave the village. The crowd began hurrying in the direction of the mountains, to make sure they got good seats in the giant theater where the crowning ceremony would take place.

# THE CORONATION OF KING JONG

Bumpo, Chee-Chee, Polynesia, Jip and I finally reached the dizzy edge of Whispering Rocks and looked down. Every man, woman and child on the island, including Long Arrow, who had been carried on his sickbed, was there.

Not a sound disturbed the solemn silence. Chills ran up and down my spine.

Accompanied by the old man, the Doctor walked up to the throne and sat down.

The old man turned around. Looking up at the people, he spoke in a quiet, even voice. Every word was heard in the farthest corner of Whispering Rocks. He recited the names of past Popsipetel Kings and spoke of the great deeds of the soon-to-be King. The old man respectfully removed the Doctor's battered high hat. He was about to put it on the ground when the Doctor grabbed it and put it in his lap.

The Sacred Crown was placed on John Dolittle's head. It did not fit very well, but it looked splendid.

"Men of Popsipetel," the man said, "behold your elected King. Are you content?"

And then the voice of the people broke loose.

*"Jong! Jong!"* they shouted. *"Long live King Jong!"*

Suddenly the old man pointed to the highest mountain, from which the Hanging Stone slowly toppled into the heart of the volcano!

"See ye, Men of the Moving Land!" the old man cried. "The King of Kings is crowned this day!"

The Doctor stood as he saw the stone fall, and expectantly looked toward the sea.

"He's thinking of the air chamber," Bumpo said in my ear.

It took a full minute for the stone to fall to the bottom of the volcano. We heard the muffled, distant thud, and then the hissing of escaping air. The Doctor's face was tense with anxiety. He sat on the throne staring out at the blue water.

Soon we felt the island slowly sinking beneath us. The sea crept inland, and the shores went down one, ten, twenty, fifty, a hundred feet! Then it stopped. Spider Monkey Island had come to rest on the bottom of the Atlantic.

The entire village of Popsipetel had disappeared, but no one was hurt. Everyone was at the coronation of King Jong. The Doctor told us later that the shouts of the people must have caused the rock to fall.

But in Popsipetel history it is believed to this day that when King Jong sat upon the throne, his mighty weight was so great that the very island sank down to honor him and never moved again.

# Part VI

# NEW POPSIPETEL

Jong Thinkalot did not sit on a throne and have people bow down to him all day. Instead, he was the busiest person I have ever seen, from early in the morning until late at night, seven days a week.

First there was the new town to be built. An entire new city of Popsipetel was planned with great care in a beautiful location at the mouth of a large river.

The Doctor showed the Indians what sewers were. He dammed a stream high in the hills and made a large lake as water supply for the town. The Indians had never seen any of these things before. Many sicknesses were prevented by proper drainage and pure drinking water.

John Dolittle searched the mountains and found iron and copper mines. He taught the Indians how the metals could be melted and made into knives, plows, water pipes and other things.

The Doctor also tried to do away with the pomp of being a King. He said if he must be King, he would be a democratic one who was friendly with his subjects. His plans for the City of New Popsipetel did not include a palace, but rather a cottage on the edge of town for himself.

That was where the Indians got involved. They were used to Kings ruling in a grand manner and insisted that he have the most magnificent palace ever built.

A thousand servants were on hand at the royal palace night and day. A royal canoe was made of polished mahogany, seventy feet long, inlaid with mother-of-pearl and paddled by the hundred strongest men on the island. The palace gardens covered a square mile.

Even in his dress the Doctor had to be formal, elegant and uncomfortable. His beloved battered high hat was put in a closet. State robes were worn on all occasions. Even when he managed to sneak off for a short natural history trip, he never dared wear his old clothes. He had to chase his butterflies with a crown upon his head and a scarlet cloak flying behind him in the wind.

There was no end to the tasks he had to perform and the questions he had to decide. In the afternoon

. . . *had to chase his butterflies with*
*a crown upon his head.*

he taught school. Grown-ups as well as children came to learn.

Bumpo and I helped with the teaching. But the Doctor taught classes in astronomy, farming and baby care himself. The Indians loved the classes. The Doctor had to take groups of five or six thousand at a time and use a megaphone to make himself heard!

Even though he didn't want to be King, John Dolittle made a very good one. Under the reign of Jong Thinkalot, Popsipetel was probably the best-ruled state in the history of the world.

The Doctor's birthday came around when we had been on the island a little more than six months. It became a great public holiday. In honor of the event, the people of the island made a tablet of ebony wood, ten feet high. It portrayed a picture history of the great events in the life of King Jong, and included verses composed by the court poet.

# THOUGHTS OF HOME

**B**umpo and I had a beautiful suite of rooms in the royal palace, which Polynesia, Jip and Chee-Chee shared with us. Officially, Bumpo was Minister of the Interior. I was First Lord of the Treasury.

One night after supper, when the Doctor was in town visiting a newborn baby, we all sat around the big table in Bumpo's reception room. We did this every evening. It was a kind of cabinet meeting.

Tonight, instead of talking of affairs of state, we were talking about England.

"When do you suppose the Doctor intends to move on from here?" Jip asked.

"Know what I think?" Polynesia said. "I believe the Doctor has given up even thinking of going home."

"Good Lord!" cried Bumpo. "No!"

"Shhh!" Polynesia said. "He's coming! Late as usual," she added. "Poor man, how he does work! Chee-Chee, get his pipe and tobacco and his dressing gown."

The Doctor looked serious as he came into the room. Wearily he took off his crown and hung it on a peg behind the door. He changed from the royal cloak to his dressing gown, dropped into his chair and filled his pipe, sighing.

Then he sat silent, staring at the ceiling through a cloud of smoke.

At last I said, "Doctor, we were wondering when you would be starting home again. Tomorrow will be seven months on the island."

The Doctor sat forward in his chair, looking uncomfortable.

"I was going to speak to you about that myself this evening," he said. "I'm afraid it would be impossible for me to leave this work now. These people have come to rely on me for a great number of things."

He thought a moment, then went on in a quieter, sadder voice, "I would like to continue my voyages and my natural history work, and I miss Puddleby as much as any of you. But I cannot close my eyes to what might happen if I leave these people and run away. They like me. They trust me. And I like *them*! I must stick to the work I took up when I assumed the crown."

"For good?" Bumpo asked. "Your whole life?"

"I don't know," the Doctor said at last.

There was a sad silence, followed by a knock at the door. The Doctor put on his crown and cloak. "Come in," he called.

A footman bowed at the entrance.

"O Kindly One, there is a traveler who wishes to see you."

"Did you ask the traveler's name?"

"Yes, Your Majesty. It is Long Arrow, the son of Golden Arrow!"

# THE RED MAN'S SCIENCE

"Long Arrow!" cried the Doctor. "How splendid! Show him in at once.

"I'm so glad," he continued, turning to us. "I've missed Long Arrow terribly. He's such a good man to have around."

It had been five months since Long Arrow had left the island in a canoe for Brazil.

When the door swung open again, there stood our friend, a smile on his strong, bronzed face. Behind him two porters carried loads packed in Indian palm matting.

"O Kindly One," Long Arrow said, "I bring you as promised the treasures of the labor of my life."

The packages were opened. Inside were many smaller packages. They were carefully laid out in rows upon the table. There were plants, flowers, fruits, leaves, roots, nuts, beans, honeys, gums, bark, seeds, bees and a few kinds of insects.

The study of plants, called botany, never interested me very much. But as Long Arrow explained his collection, I became fascinated. Soon I was totally absorbed by the wonders he had brought.

"These," he said, taking up a little packet of big seeds, "are what I call 'laughing beans.'"

While Long Arrow's back was turned, Bumpo popped three of the beans into his mouth and swallowed them.

"Alas," said Long Arrow when he discovered what Bumpo had done. "He should not have eaten more than a quarter of one seed. Let us hope he does not die laughing."

The beans' effect on Bumpo was extraordinary. In minutes he broke into a broad smile; then he began to giggle. Finally he burst into such hearty roars of laughter, we had to carry him out and put him to bed.

The Doctor said Bumpo could have died from laughter had he not been so strong. All night he gurgled happily in his sleep. When we woke him next morning he rolled out of bed still chuckling.

When we returned to the reception room, we saw red roots that, when made into soup with sugar and salt, caused people to dance with great speed. He asked if we wanted to try them, but we politely refused. After seeing Bumpo, we were afraid of any more experiments.

There was no end to the strange and useful things Long Arrow had collected: oil that would make hair grow in one night; an orange as big as a pumpkin raised in his own garden in Peru; black honey that would put you to sleep and make you awaken fresh in the morning; a nut to make the voice beautiful for singing; waterweed that stopped cuts from bleeding; moss that cured snakebite; and lichen to prevent seasickness.

The Doctor was terribly excited. As Long Arrow dictated, he wrote down in his notebook the name and description of each item.

"Stubbins," he said, his voice sounding more the way it did in Puddleby. "There are things here that in the hands of skilled druggists could make a vast difference in medicine and chemistry. Miranda was right: Long Arrow is a great naturalist. Someday I must get these things to England. But when?" he added sadly. "When?"

# THE SEA SERPENT

For a long time after that meeting, we did not discuss going home. Life on Spider Monkey Island went along. The winter came and went. Summer was with us before we knew it.

As time passed, the Doctor became even busier. The hours he could spare for his natural history work grew fewer. When something reminded him of England or his old life, his face grew thoughtful and a little sad. But he never spoke of it. I believe he would have spent the rest of his days on the island if it hadn't been for an accident and for Polynesia.

One morning Polynesia and I were watching the Doctor oversee the building of a new theater in Popsipetel. There were already an opera house and a concert hall. Polynesia got so annoyed at the sight, I suggested we take a walk.

"Do you really think," I asked as we sat on the sand, "that he will never go back to Puddleby again?"

"I don't know," she groaned. "I've been racking my brains to think up a plan. If we could only hit upon something that would turn his thoughts back to natural history again . . . something big enough to get him excited . . . we might manage it. But how?"

I lay on the warm beach, thinking of my mother and father. Polynesia kept muttering beside me. Listening to the lapping waves, I fell asleep, and had a dream. In it, the island moved again. It moved suddenly, as though something powerful had heaved it up and dropped it down. I was awakened by Polynesia's gentle pecking on my nose.

"Tommy! What a boy! You slept through an earthquake and never noticed it!"

"What's the matter?" I said, yawning as I sat up.

"Shhh! Look! Here's our chance now," whispered Polynesia, pointing out to sea.

Not more than thirty yards from shore, I saw an enormous pale pink shell. Dome-shaped, it towered up in a graceful rainbow curve to a tremendous height.

"What in the world is it?" I asked.

"That," she whispered, "is what sailors call the sea serpent. I've seen it from the decks of ships, from far away. But now that I see it up close, I think that the sea serpent is none other than the great glass sea snail the fidgit told us about! Tommy, we're in luck. We must get the Doctor down here to see it before it moves off to the Deep Hole. If we can, we may leave this blessed island yet. Stay here and keep an eye on it. I'll get the Doctor. Don't move or speak; it might get scared. Snails are awful timid things."

Creeping up the sands, Polynesia hid behind some bushes before flying toward town. I waited alone on the shore and watched this unbelievable monster in fascination.

It moved very little. It seemed to be hurt.

Polynesia returned with the Doctor. They were so silent, I didn't know they were there until they crouched beside me in the sand.

One sight of the snail changed the Doctor completely. His eyes sparkled with delight. I hadn't seen him so thrilled since he caught the jabizri beetle when we first landed on the island.

"The great glass sea snail himself!" he whispered. "Polynesia, see if you can find any porpoises. Perhaps they'll know why the snail is here. It's unusual for him to be in such shallow water. Stubbins, you go to the harbor and get a canoe. Be careful to paddle quietly so you don't frighten him."

"And don't tell any of the Indians," Polynesia added in a whisper as I moved to go. "We must keep this a secret or we'll have a crowd of sight-seers here in five minutes."

I reached the harbor and took a small, light canoe.

Polynesia returned ahead of me with a pair of porpoises. These were already conversing in low tones with John Dolittle.

"What I want to know," the Doctor was saying, "is how the snail comes here. I thought he always stayed in the Deep Hole or else surfaced in midocean."

"Oh, haven't you heard?" the porpoises replied. "You covered up the Deep Hole when you sank the island. The fishes that were in it at the time have been trying to get out ever since. The great snail had the worst luck of all—he was nipped in the tail just as he was leaving the Hole. It took him six months to wriggle free. He finally heaved the whole island up at one end to get his tail loose. Didn't you feel a sort of earthquake about an hour ago?"

"I did!" the Doctor said. "It shook down part of the theater I'm building."

"Well, that was the snail. All the other fishes escaped when he raised the lid. But the strain of the heave sprained a muscle in his tail."

"Dear me!" said the Doctor. "I'm terribly sorry. It was an accident that the island was let down. Is the poor fellow hurt very badly?"

"We're not sure, because none of us can speak the language. He doesn't seem seriously injured."

"Can't any of your people speak shellfish?" the Doctor asked.

"Not a word. It's a difficult language."

"Could you find some fish who could?"

"We could try," said the porpoises.

"I'd be extremely grateful," said the Doctor. "There are so many important questions I want to ask this snail."

"Wait here," the porpoises said. "We'll see what we can do."

# THE SHELLFISH RIDDLE SOLVED AT LAST

S o Doctor Dolittle waited upon the shore. The porpoises shuttled back and forth for an hour, bringing different sea creatures to see if they could help.

But it seemed that very few spoke shellfish. The porpoises were hopeful when they found a sea urchin who said he understood starfish, but not pure shellfish. The urchin stayed with us while the porpoises went looking for a starfish.

They were back quickly and, using the sea urchin as an interpreter, questioned the starfish.

We found he could speak shellfish fairly well.

Encouraged, the Doctor and I got into the canoe. The porpoises, urchin and starfish swam alongside.

Paddling very gently, we stopped under the towering shell of the great snail.

Then began the strangest conversation. First the starfish asked the snail something. The snail gave the answer to the urchin, who told the porpoises, who told the Doctor.

The Doctor was very excited about getting so close to learning the language he had so longed to know. Soon, by having the other fish repeat short phrases the snail used, he began to put words together himself. The Doctor was already familiar with several other fish languages, which helped a great deal. He practiced for a while, then put his face below the water and tried speaking directly to the snail.

It was very difficult, and it took hours to get any results. But I could tell by the happy look on the Doctor's face that he was making progress.

The sun was low in the west when the Doctor turned to me. "Stubbins," he said, "I have persuaded the snail to come onto dry land and let me examine his tail. Go to the palace and get my medicine bag. It's under the throne in the Audience Chamber."

When I returned, the snail was on the beach. Seeing his size, it was easy to understand why sailors called him the sea serpent. John Dolittle examined the swelling on his tail.

Doctor Dolittle took a large bottle from the bag I brought and began rubbing the sprain with its contents. Then he took all the bandages he had and fastened them end to end. Even then, they were not long enough to get more than halfway around the snail's huge tail. Insisting that the swelling must be strapped tight, he sent me back to the palace to get every sheet from the Royal Linen Closet. Polynesia and I tied these into bandages for him. At last he was satisfied that the sprain was well strapped.

The snail was delighted by all the attention. He stretched himself on the beach in comfort. When the shell on his back was empty, we could look right through it.

"One of us had better sit up with him tonight," the Doctor said. "I'll ask Bumpo. He's been napping in the summerhouse all day. If I wasn't so busy, I would stay. I still have so many things to talk over with him!" He sighed.

"You know, Doctor," Polynesia said as we prepared to go back to town, "you ought to take a holiday. All Kings take holidays once in a while."

"I suppose that's true," said the Doctor.

"I tell you what to do," she said, trying not to sound as excited as she felt. "When you get back to the palace, publish a proclamation that you are going away for a week into the country for your health, *without any servants*, just like a plain person. They all do it . . . It's called *traveling incognito*. Then the week you're away, you can rest on the beach. And talk to the snail!"

"It sounds most attractive," the Doctor agreed. "But there is so much work to be done with the theater. And the native mothers need my help!"

"Oh, bother the theater—and the babies too," snapped Polynesia. "Take a holiday. You need it! And I do too!"

# THE LAST CABINET MEETING

The Doctor and I walked silently back to the palace. I could see that Polynesia's words had made an impression on him.

After supper he disappeared from the palace without saying a word. We all knew he had gone back to the beach to be with the snail. He never even mentioned it to Bumpo.

As soon as the doors were closed, Polynesia said, "This is our last chance. We've got to get the Doctor to take this holiday or we'll be on this island for the rest of our blessed lives."

"What difference will the holiday make?" Bumpo asked.

"Don't you see?" Polynesia said to him impatiently. "If he has a whole week to get into his natural history stuff again, he might agree to leave this island. But while he is King he never gets a moment to think about anything but government."

"That's true," Bumpo agreed.

"Besides," Polynesia added, "the only way he could ever escape here is secretly. He's got to leave while on holiday. The Indians would never let him go. If we get him to agree to the holiday, we must get the sea snail to promise to take us in his shell to the mouth of Puddleby River. The temptation will be too great for the Doctor to pass up. I know he'll come, because he can take this chance to see the bottom of the ocean floor and bring Long Arrow's medicines back to England with him."

"How thrilling!" I cried. "Do you mean the snail could take us all the way back to Puddleby under the sea?"

"Of course," Polynesia said. "He could crawl along the ocean floor and the Doctor could see all the sights."

"I hope the Doctor agrees," Jip said. "I'm sick of the tropics. There are no rats here to chase or anything! And wouldn't Dab-Dab be glad to have us back!"

"By the end of next month it will be two whole years since we left England," I said. "Since we pulled up anchor at Kingsbridge and bumped our way out into the river. Do you remember all the people waving from the river wall?"

"Yes. And I suppose they've often wondered whether we're dead or alive," Jip added.

"Cease!" Bumpo said. "I feel I am about to weep from sediment!"

# THE DOCTOR'S DECISION

After his all-night talk with the snail, the Doctor made up his mind to take a holiday. A proclamation was published right away that His Majesty was going to the country for a seven-day rest. During his absence, the palace and government offices would be open as usual.

Polynesia was thrilled. She set to work quietly planning every part of the departure. She made sure no one knew where we were going or what we were taking.

Polynesia told me I must take *all* the Doctor's notebooks. Long Arrow, the only Indian let in on the secret, said he would like to come as far as the beach to see the great snail. Polynesia told him to bring his plants so the Doctor could bring them to England. Bumpo was ordered to carry the high hat, carefully hidden under his coat. We were to leave at midnight, when most townspeople would be asleep.

When the clock struck twelve, we stepped silently into the moonlit garden. No one had seen us leave.

Something made me pause and look back before we reached the beach. I knew we were leaving never to return. I wondered what other Kings and ministers would live and rule in the palace when we were gone. I hoped they would be as kind as King Jong.

At the beach, we found the snail feeling much better. He could move his tail with no pain. The porpoises were still hanging about to see what was happening. While the Doctor was checking the snail's tail, Polynesia pulled them aside for a private chat.

"My friends," she said, "you know how much John Dolittle has done for the animals. Here is your chance to do something for him. He was made King of this island against his will. Now he feels he cannot leave, which is nonsense. Here's your job. I need you to tell the sea urchin to tell the starfish to tell the snail to take us in his shell to Puddleby River. Is that plain?"

"Quite," said the porpoises. "We will do our best to persuade him. It is a shame for the great man to waste his time here when he is so needed by the animals."

"But don't let the Doctor know what you're up to," she warned. "Get the snail to offer on his own account to take us."

Half an hour passed. It seemed like a very long time.

*The porpoises were still hanging about.*

Suddenly the Doctor left the snail and **splashed** out to us breathlessly.

"What *do* you think?" he cried excitedly. "**The** snail has offered, on his very own, to take us all **back to Eng**-land inside his shell. He says he has to take a **voyage of** discovery to find a new home, since the **Deep Hole is** closed. It wouldn't be out of his way to get to the **mouth** of Puddleby River! Goodness, what a chance! No man has ever examined the ocean floor all the way from Brazil to Europe! . . . Oh, that I had never allowed myself to be made King! Now the chance of my lifetime will slip by!"

No one said a word. Doctor Dolittle turned and moved to the middle of the beach, gazing longingly at the snail.

Polynesia rose and quietly moved to his side.

"Doctor," she said in a soft voice, as though speaking to a child. "This King business is not your real work in life. The natives will manage, not as well as with you, but they will learn. You have done your duty by them and taught them well. Accept the snail's offer. The work you'll do, the information you'll carry home, will be of more lasting value than what is here. The people will continue your work, I am sure."

"Good friend," the Doctor said sadly, "I cannot. I fear they will go back to their old ways. Something else will turn up."

"That is where you are wrong, Doctor," she said. "Now is when you should go. Nothing will 'turn up.' The longer you stay, the harder it will be to leave. Go tonight!"

The Doctor stood thinking silently.

"There are my notebooks," he said.

"I have all of them here, Doctor," I said, speaking up.

"And Long Arrow's collection!"

"It is here, O Kindly One," came the Indian's deep voice from a shadow beneath the palm.

"Provisions?" asked the Doctor. "Food for the journey?"

"We have a week's supply for the holiday," said Polynesia. "That's more than we need."

The Doctor stood silent and thoughtful.

"My hat!" he said fretfully. "How could I appear in Puddleby with this crown on my head?"

"Here it is, Doctor," Bumpo said, pulling the old hat from beneath his coat.

But we could tell the Doctor was still trying to think up more excuses.

"O Kindly One," said Long Arrow, "why tempt ill fortune? Your way is clear. Your future and your work beckon you back to your home. And you will share what I have gathered for mankind in lands where it will be of wider use than here. Day is at hand. Go now. For truly I believe that unless you do, you will remain the captive King of the Popsipetels."

Great decisions are made in a short time. The Doctor suddenly lifted the Sacred Crown from his head and laid it on the sands.

"They will find it here," he murmured, his voice choked with tears. "And they will know I have gone. Will they ever understand or forgive me?"

He took his old hat from Bumpo. Facing Long Arrow, he gripped the Indian's outstretched hand in silence.

"You do right, O Kindly One," Long Arrow said. "Farewell. May good fortune ever lead you by the hand."

It was the only time I ever saw the Doctor weep. Without a word, he turned and headed into the shallow water of the sea.

The snail made an opening between his shoulders and the edge of his shell. The Doctor climbed up and in. We followed him with our baggage. The opening shut tight with a whistling noise.

The great creature turned east and slowly moved forward, sloping into deeper waters. As the swirling dark green waters closed above our heads, the sun popped up over the ocean. And through the snail's transparent shell, we saw the world beneath the sea light up with daybreak.

The story of our homeward voyage is brief, compared to our two-year adventure, but extraordinarily exciting. Inside the spacious shell, the snail's wide back was quite comfortable. He just asked us to remove our boots because the hobnails hurt his back as we ran from side to side, looking at the sights.

I had always thought that the bottom of the sea was flat. I found it was as bumpy as dry land. There were mountain ranges, dense forests of tall sea plants, and empty stretches of sandy mud, like deserts.

In the lower levels we often passed the shadowy shapes of dead ships. In the deeper, darker water, monstrous fish would spring up suddenly, then flash away with the speed of an arrow. Bolder ones came up and peered at *us* through the shell! It was a thrilling and ever-changing show.

The Doctor wrote and sketched without stopping, filling every blank notebook we had left. It was hard to get light to see for writing. It was very dim in the lower waters. On the third day, a band of fire eels passed. The Doctor asked them to swim alongside us for light.

During the darkness of night the snail swam, rather than crawled, making terrific speed just by waggling his long tail. We completed the entire journey in five and a half days!

Early in the afternoon of the sixth day, we felt we were climbing a gentle slope and noticed that it was growing lighter. We saw that the snail had crawled out of the water and had stopped on a long strip of sand.

Behind us, the surface of the sea rippled. On our left was the mouth of a river. In front, low, flat land stretched into the mist. It was a great change from the hot sunshine of Popsipetel!

With the same whistling sound, the snail made an opening for us to crawl out. We stepped upon the marshy land and noticed a fine, autumn rain drizzling.

"Can this be Merrie England?" Bumpo asked. "Doesn't look like any place in particular with the mist."

"Yes," said Polynesia, shaking the rain off her feathers. "This is England. You can tell by the beastly climate."

"Oh!" cried Jip, as he sniffed up gulps of air. "But it has a *smell*—a good and glorious smell! I see a water rat!" And off he went.

"Shhh! Listen!" said Chee-Chee through teeth chattering from the cold. "There's Puddleby Church striking four."

"Let's hope that Dab-Dab has a nice fire burning in the kitchen," I said. We said goodbye to the snail and headed across the marshes.

"I'm sure she will," said the Doctor. He picked out his old bag from among the bundles. "Come along. Let's hug the riverbank so we don't miss our way in the fog."

He sighed and looked around, smiling. "You know, there's something rather attractive about the bad weather in England—when you've a kitchen fire to look forward to. Four o'clock! Come along—we'll just be in time for tea!"

THE END

# ABOUT THE AUTHOR

Hugh Lofting was born in Maidenhead, England, in 1886 and was educated at home with his brothers and sister until he was eight. He studied engineering in London and at the Massachusetts Institute of Technology. After his marriage in 1912 he settled in the United States.

During World War I he left his job as a civil engineer, was commissioned a lieutenant in the Irish Guards, and found that writing illustrated letters to his children eased the strain of war. "There seemed to be very little to write to youngsters from the front; the news was either too horrible or too dull. One thing that kept forcing itself more and more upon my attention was the very considerable part the animals were playing in the war. That was the beginning of an idea: an eccentric country physician with a bent for natural history and a great love of pets . . ."

These letters became *The Story of Doctor Dolittle*, published in 1920. Children all over the world have read this book and the eleven that followed, for they have been translated into almost every language. *The Voyages of Doctor Dolittle* won the Newbery Medal in 1923. Drawing from the twelve Doctor Dolittle volumes, Hugh Lofting's sister-in-law, Olga Fricker, later compiled *Doctor Dolittle: A Treasury,* which was published by Dell in 1986 as a Yearling Classic.

Hugh Lofting died in 1947 at his home in Topanga, California.